序　言

　　自「全民英檢」初級測驗實施以來，參加考試的人數逐年增加，顯示國人越來越重視這項檢定考試。我們的「**初級英語聽力檢定①②③④**」，以及「**初級英語模擬試題①②③④**」出版之後，受到讀者廣大的迴響，許多國中都集體訂購這兩套書，當作教科書使用，給了我們非常大的鼓勵。

　　因此，我們再推出「**初級英語聽力檢定⑤**」，書中所有的內容，均由本公司美籍老師親筆撰寫，用字遣詞最接近美國人的說法。同學們做練習之餘，還可以模仿 CD 中外國人說話的語氣，大聲地朗讀句子，以熟悉各類句型的語調，增加語感，爲初檢複試的「口說能力測驗」暖身。

　　本書共收錄 12 回聽力測驗，所有試題均附有詳細的中文翻譯及單字註解，節省讀者查字典的時間。考聽力的時候，建議同學可以先看選項，再聽題目，遇到題目聽不懂時，要趕快放棄，先看下一題，絕對要超前錄音帶的內容，先看選項，不能落後；此外，可能會出現三個選項都與問題相關，所以要聽清楚題目的重點，及其所使用的動詞時態；再者，要有開放的心胸，把「醫生都是男的；只有女生才會煮飯」的傳統觀念丟掉，否則它可能會擾亂同學在第三部份「簡短（男女）對話」的作答。掌握上述原則，就可掌握得分關鍵！

　　本書雖經審慎的編校，疏漏之處恐在所難免，誠盼各界先進不吝給予批評指正。

劉　毅

全民英語能力分級檢定測驗
初級測驗①

本測驗分三部份，全為三選一之選擇題，每部份各 10 題，共 30 題，作答時間約 20 分鐘。

第一部份：看圖辨義

本部份共 10 題，試題冊上每題有一個圖片，請聽錄音機播出一個相關的問題，與 A、B、C 三個英語敘述後，選一個與所看到圖片最相符的答案，並在答案紙上相對的圓圈內塗黑作答。每題播出一遍，問題及選項均不印在試題冊上。

例：（看）

NT$80   NT$50

（聽）

Look at the picture. How much is the hamburger?

   A. It's eighty dollars.
   B. It's fifty-five dollars.
   C. It's eighteen dollars.

正確答案為 A

A. **Question 1**

B. **Question 2**

C. **Question 3**

D. <u>Question 4</u>

E. <u>Question 5-6</u>

請 翻 頁 ⟹

F. Question 7

G. Question 8

H. Question 9

I. Question 10

請翻頁 ▯▭▷

第二部份： 問答

本部份共 10 題，每題錄音機會播出一個問句或直述句，每題播出一次，聽後請從試題冊上 A、B、C 三個選項中，選出一個最適合的回答或回應，並在答案紙上塗黑作答。

例：

（聽） Good morning, Kevin. How are you?

（看） A. I'm fine, thank you.
　　　B. I'm in the living room.
　　　C. My name is Kevin.

正確答案為 A

11. A. It's in May.
　　B. In 1991.
　　C. Happy birthday!

12. A. I'll have a Coke with that.
　　B. Yes, I do.
　　C. No, thank you.

13. A. Oh, yes! It was a lot of fun!
　　B. There were hippos and lions.
　　C. I went with Tim.

14. A. I'll close the window.
　　B. Yes. I don't feel well.
　　C. Of course I am. It's winter!

15. A. That's all right.
    B. You're welcome.
    C. Help yourself.

16. A. I like to roller-
       skate.
    B. Because it's a very
       big park.
    C. Whenever I can.

17. A. It's Monday.
    B. It's October 9th.
    C. I have a date with
       Jim today.

18. A. It was delicious.
    B. It's over there.
    C. I thought it was
       fantastic!

19. A. In that apartment
       building.
    B. She is fourteen.
    C. To Keelung.

20. A. I can't. I don't have
       a spoon.
    B. Here you are.
    C. Don't mention it.

請 翻 頁

第三部份： 簡短對話

本部份共 10 題，每題錄音機會播出一段對話及一個相關的問題，每題播出兩次，聽後請從試題冊上 A、B、C 三個選項中，選出一個最適合的回答，並在答案紙上塗黑作答。

例：

(聽) (Woman) Good afternoon, …Mr. Davis?

(Man) Yes. I have an appointment with Dr. Sanders at two o'clock. My son Tommy has a fever.

(Woman) Oh, that's too bad. Well, please have a seat, Mr. Davis. Dr. Sanders will be right with you.

Question: Where did this conversation take place?

(看) A. In a post office.

B. In a restaurant.

C. In a doctor's office.

正確答案為 C

21. A. People should drive
    their cars less often.

    B. Most people would
    rather pay more
    money than walk.

    C. It will cost more to
    buy gas.

22. A. He forgot the phone
    number of the person
    he wanted to call.

    B. He didn't know how
    to make a long-
    distance call by
    himself.

    C. He wanted to know
    her telephone number.

23. A. He bought two kilos
    of apples.

    B. He bought two
    apples.

    C. He bought 100
    apples.

24. A. A card.

    B. Some flowers.

    C. A cake.

25. A. She has three
    brothers.

    B. She is the oldest
    child in her family.

    C. She is younger than
    her brothers.

請 翻 頁 ▯⟹

26. A. She is too young to
count.
B. She is only in second
grade.
C. She is a good singer.

27. A. The woman doesn't
want to go.
B. The weather is too bad.
C. They are too busy.

28. A. He will learn to use a
computer.
B. He will play music well.
C. He will learn how to
play an instrument.

29. A. Chicken, rice and
potatoes.
B. Potatoes or French
fries.
C. Chicken with
French fries.

30. A. They are at a
concert.
B. They are at a
restaurant.
C. They are at a
hospital.

初級英語聽力檢定①詳解

第一部份

For question number 1, please look at picture A.

1. (**B**) What are the man and the woman doing?

    A. She is going to sleep.

    B. They are talking on the telephone.

    C. They are in love.

    * sleep〔slip〕v. 睡覺　　*talk on the telephone* 講電話
    be in love 在談戀愛

For question number 2, please look at picture B.

2. (**C**) What are those people doing in the park?

    A. They are walking their dog.

    B. They are late for class.

    C. They are jogging.

    * walk〔wɔk〕v. 遛（狗）　　late〔let〕adj. 遲到的
    jog〔dʒɑg〕v. 慢跑

For question number 3, please look at picture C.

3. (**B**) Why are they running?

    A. It is too hot.

    B. They are late.

    C. They are exercising.

    * run〔rʌn〕v. 跑　　exercise〔'ɛksɚ,saɪz〕v. 運動

For question number 4, please look at picture D.

4. (**C**)　What kind of novel is the girl reading?
　　　　　A.　A boring novel.
　　　　　B.　A funny novel.
　　　　　C.　A sad novel.

　　　　* kind〔kaɪnd〕*n.* 種類　　novel〔'nɑvḷ〕*n.* 小說
　　　　　boring〔'borɪŋ〕*adj.* 無聊的
　　　　　funny〔'fʌnɪ〕*adj.* 好笑的
　　　　　sad〔sæd〕*adj.* 悲傷的

For question number 5 and 6, please look at picture E.

5. (**B**)　How many nieces does Jack have?
　　　　　A.　One.
　　　　　B.　Two.
　　　　　C.　Three.

　　　　* niece〔nis〕*n.* 姪女；外甥女

6. (**C**)　Please look at picture E again.　How many cousins
　　　　　does Sam have?
　　　　　A.　One.
　　　　　B.　Two.
　　　　　C.　Three.

　　　　* cousin〔'kʌzn̩〕*n.* 表（堂）兄弟姊妹

For question number 7, please look at picture F.

7. (**B**) Where are the man and woman?

    A. They are sitting down.

    B. They are on a bench.

    C. They are holding hands.

    * *sit down* 坐下   bench〔bɛntʃ〕*n.* 長椅

     hold〔hold〕*v.* 握

For question number 8, please look at picture G.

8. (**C**) What is player A doing?

    A. He is on team X.

    B. He is hitting a homerun.

    C. He is running to second base.

    * player〔'pleɚ〕*n.* 球員   team〔tim〕*n.* 隊

     hit〔hɪt〕*v.* 擊出   homerun〔'hom,rʌn〕*n.* 全壘打

     second base 二壘

For question number 9, please look at picture H.

9. (**A**) What is hanging on the clothesline?

    A. There is a T-shirt.

    B. They are drying.

    C. There are two clouds.

    * hang〔hæŋ〕*v.* 懸掛;吊

     clothesline〔'kloz,laɪn〕*n.* 曬衣繩

     T-shirt〔'ti,ʃɜt〕*n.* T恤

     dry〔draɪ〕*v.* 曬乾   cloud〔klaʊd〕*n.* 雲

For question number 10, please look at picture I.

10. (**B**) What are the two people doing?

    A. They are writing a letter.

    B. They are saying good-bye.

    C. They are traveling by bus.

    * good-bye〔gud'baɪ〕*interj.* 再見（= *goodbye* = *bye*）

       travel〔'trævl̩〕*v.* 旅行

第二部份

11. (**B**) When were you born?

    A. It's in May.   B. In 1991.

    C. Happy birthday!

    * born〔bɔrn〕*adj.* 出生的   May〔me〕*n.* 五月

12. (**C**) Would you like some popcorn?

    A. I'll have a Coke with that.

    B. Yes, I do.   C. No, thank you.

    * ***Would you like ～?*** 你要不要～？

       popcorn〔'pɑp,kɔrn〕*n.* 爆米花

       Coke〔kok〕*n.* 可口可樂

13. (**B**) What did you see at the zoo?

    A. Oh, yes! It was a lot of fun!

    B. There were hippos and lions.

    C. I went with Tim.

    * zoo〔zu〕*n.* 動物園   fun〔fʌn〕*n.* 樂趣

       hippo〔'hɪpo〕*n.* 河馬   lion〔'laɪən〕*n.* 獅子

14. (**B**) Do you have a cold?

A. I'll close the window.

B. Yes. I don't feel well.

C. Of course I am. It's winter!

* cold〔kold〕*n.* 感冒　　window〔'wɪndo〕*n.* 窗戶
feel〔fil〕*v.* 覺得　　well〔wɛl〕*adj.* 健康的
of course 當然　　winter〔'wɪntɚ〕*n.* 冬天

15. (**A**) I want to apologize for my mistake.

A. That's all right.

B. You're welcome.

C. Help yourself.

* apologize〔ə'pɑləˌdʒaɪz〕*v.* 道歉
mistake〔mə'stek〕*n.* 錯誤
That's all right. 沒關係。
You are welcome. 不客氣。
Help yourself. 隨意取用（食物等）。

16. (**A**) What do you like to do at the park?

A. I like to roller-skate.

B. Because it's a very big park.

C. Whenever I can.

* roller-skate〔'rolɚˌsket〕*v.* 穿輪鞋溜冰
whenever〔hwɛn'ɛvɚ〕*adv.* 無論何時

17. (**B**) What's the date today?

    A. It's Monday.

    B. It's October 9th.

    C. I have a date with Jim today.

    * date〔det〕*n.* 日期；（男女）約會

      Monday〔'mʌndɪ, -de〕*n.* 星期一

      October〔ɑk'tobɚ〕*n.* 十月

      have a date with *sb.* 與某人有（男女）約會

18. (**C**) How did you like the movie?

    A. It was delicious.

    B. It's over there.

    C. I thought it was fantastic!

    * ***How do you like ~?*** 你覺得～怎麼樣；你喜歡～嗎？

      delicious〔dɪ'lɪʃəs〕*adj.* 美味的

      over there 在那裡

      think〔θɪŋk〕*v.* 認為（三態變化為：think-thought-thought）

      fantastic〔fæn'tæstɪk〕*adj.* 很棒的

19. (**A**) Where does Alice live?

    A. In that apartment building.

    B. She is fourteen.

    C. To Keelung.

    * live〔lɪv〕*v.* 住

      apartment〔ə'partmənt〕*n.* 公寓

      building〔'bɪldɪŋ〕*n.* 建築物；大樓

      fourteen〔for'tin〕*n.* 十四歲

      Keelung〔'ki'lʌŋ〕*n.* 基隆

20. (**B**)　Please pass the soup.
　　　　　A. I can't. I don't have a spoon.
　　　　　B. Here you are.　　　C. Don't mention it.

　　　　　* pass〔pæs〕v. 傳遞　　　soup〔sup〕n. 湯
　　　　　spoon〔spun〕n. 湯匙
　　　　　Here you are. 你要的東西在這裡；拿去吧。(= *Here it is.*)
　　　　　mention〔'mɛnʃən〕v. 提起 (事)
　　　　　Don't mention it. 不客氣。

第三部份

21. (**C**)　M：Did you see this story in the newspaper?
　　　　　W：No. What's it about?
　　　　　M：It says that the price of gas is going up.
　　　　　W：Maybe we can drive the car less often.
　　　　　M：No way! I'd rather pay more money than walk!
　　　　　Question：What did the newspaper story say?
　　　　　A. People should drive their cars less often.
　　　　　B. Most people would rather pay more money than
　　　　　　walk.
　　　　　C. It will cost more to buy gas.

　　　　　* story〔'storɪ〕n. 報導　　newspaper〔'njuz,pepɚ〕n. 報紙
　　　　　price〔praɪs〕n. 價格　　gas〔gæs〕n. 汽油 (= *gasoline*)
　　　　　go up　(物價) 上漲　maybe〔'mebɪ〕adv. 可能；或許
　　　　　drive〔draɪv〕v. 駕駛　　less〔lɛs〕adv. 更少
　　　　　often〔'ɔfən〕adv. 經常　　***No way!*** 不行！
　　　　　would rather…than ~ 寧願…，也不願~
　　　　　pay〔pe〕v. 支付　　cost〔kɔst〕v. 花費 (錢)

22. (**B**) M: Operator, I'd like to make a long-distance call.

W: Which city?

M: Chicago.

W: Number, please.

M: 408-6767.

Question: Why did the man call the operator?

A. He forgot the phone number of the person he wanted to call.

B. He didn't know how to make a long-distance call by himself.

C. He wanted to know her telephone number.

* operator〔'ɑpəˌretə〕 n. 接線生

would like to V. 想要～ (= want to V.)

make a long-distance call 打長途電話

long-distance〔'lɔŋ'dɪstəns〕 adj. 長途的

city〔'sɪtɪ〕 n. 城市

number〔'nʌmbə〕 n. 電話號碼 (= phone number)

forget〔fə'gɛt〕 v. 忘記

by oneself 自己

23. (**A**) M: How much are the apples?

W: They're NT$50 a kilo.

M: I'll take two.

W: That'll be NT$100.

Question: What did the man buy?

A. He bought two kilos of apples.

B. He bought two apples.

C. He bought 100 apples.

* kilo〔'kɪlo〕*n.* 公斤（＝kilogram〔'kɪlə͵græm〕）

take〔tek〕*v.* 買

buy〔baɪ〕*v.* 買（三態變化為：buy-bought-bought）

24.（ **C** ） M：Happy birthday, Mom!

W：Thank you, dear.

M：This is for you.

W：Oh, it looks delicious!

Question：What did the boy give his mother?

A. A card.

B. Some flowers.

C. A cake.

* mom〔mɑm〕*n.* 媽媽

dear〔dɪr〕*n.* 親愛的（用於稱呼）

look〔lʊk〕*v.* 看起來

delicious〔dɪ'lɪʃəs〕*adj.* 美味的

card〔kɑrd〕*n.* 卡片　　flower〔'flaʊɚ〕*n.* 花

cake〔kek〕*n.* 蛋糕

25. (**B**)　M：How many children are there in your family?

W：Three.　My two brothers and me.

M：Are they older or younger?

W：They are both younger than me.

Question：What do we know about the woman?

A.　She has three brothers.

B.　She is the oldest child in her family.

C.　She is younger than her brothers.

* children〔'tʃɪldrən〕 *n. pl.* 小孩（child 的複數）

　　old〔old〕*adj.* 老的　　young〔jʌŋ〕*adj.* 年輕的

　　both〔boθ〕*adj.* 兩者的　　child〔tʃaɪld〕*n.* 小孩

26. (**A**)　M：Can your sister count to 10?

W：No, she is only two years old.

M：Can she sing a song?

W：Yes, she can.

Question：What does the girl say about her sister?

A.　She is too young to count.

B.　She is only in second grade.

C.　She is a good singer.

* count〔kaʊnt〕 *v.* 數（數）

　　sing〔sɪŋ〕 *v.* 唱（歌）　　song〔sɔŋ〕 *n.* 歌

　　too…to～　太…以致不能～

　　second〔'sɛkənd〕 *adj.* 第二的

　　grade〔gred〕 *n.* 年級　　singer〔'sɪŋɚ〕 *n.* 歌手

27. (**B**)　M：Would you like to go on a picnic today?

　　　W：Sure, but we can't.

　　　M：Why not?　Are you too busy?

　　　W：No.　It's raining.

　　Question：Why can't they go on the picnic?

　　A. The woman doesn't want to go.

　　B. The weather is too bad.

　　C. They are too busy.

　　* ***go on a picnic*** 去野餐　　sure〔ʃʊr〕*adv.* 好；當然
　　busy〔'bɪzɪ〕*adj.* 忙的　　rain〔ren〕*v.* 下雨
　　weather〔'wɛðɚ〕*n.* 天氣　　bad〔bæd〕*adj.* 不好的

28. (**C**)　M：Are you going to camp this summer?

　　　W：Yes.　I'm going to a computer camp.

　　　M：That sounds interesting.　I'm going to music camp.

　　　W：Are you good at music?

　　　M：No, but I want to learn to play the guitar.

　　Question：What will the man do this summer?

　　A. He will learn to use a computer.

　　B. He will play music well.

　　C. He will learn how to play an instrument.

　　* camp〔kæmp〕*v.* 露營　*n.* 營隊
　　computer〔kəm'pjutɚ〕*n.* 電腦
　　sound〔saʊnd〕*v.* 聽起來　　music〔'mjuzɪk〕*n.* 音樂
　　interesting〔'ɪntrɪstɪŋ〕*adj.* 有趣的　　***be good at*** 擅長
　　play〔ple〕*v.* 彈；演奏　　guitar〔gɪ'tɑr〕*n.* 吉他
　　instrument〔'ɪnstrəmənt〕*n.* 樂器

29. (**C**) M: What would you like with your chicken, rice or potatoes?

W: Do you have French fries?

M: Yes, we do.

W: Then I'll have the French fries.

Question: What did the woman order?

A. Chicken, rice and potatoes.

B. Potatoes or French fries.

C. Chicken with French fries.

* with〔wɪθ〕*prep.* 和⋯一起　　chicken〔'tʃɪkən〕*n.* 雞肉
  rice〔raɪs〕*n.* 米飯　　potato〔pə'teto〕*n.* 馬鈴薯
  French fries 薯條　　have〔hæv〕*v.* 吃
  order〔'ɔrdɚ〕*v.* 點（菜）

30. (**B**) M: Where's Dave?

W: He couldn't come. He has a cold.

M: That's too bad. We should order some extra pizza and take it to him.

W: I think he'd like that.

Question: Where are they?

A. They are at a concert.

B. They are at a restaurant.

C. They are at a hospital.

* ***have a cold*** 感冒　　***That's too bad.*** 眞糟糕。
  extra〔'ɛkstrə〕*adj.* 額外的　　pizza〔'pitsə〕*n.* 披薩
  concert〔'kɑnsɝt〕*n.* 音樂會
  restaurant〔'rɛstərənt〕*n.* 餐廳
  hospital〔'hɑspɪtl̩〕*n.* 醫院

全民英語能力分級檢定測驗

初級測驗 ②

　　本測驗分三部份，全為三選一之選擇題，每部份各 10 題，共 30 題，作答時間約 20 分鐘。

第一部份：看圖辨義

　　　　　本部份共 10 題，試題冊上每題有一個圖片，請聽錄音機播出一個相關的問題，與 A、B、C 三個英語敘述後，選一個與所看到圖片最相符的答案，並在答案紙上相對的圓圈內塗黑作答。每題播出一遍，問題及選項均不印在試題冊上。

例：（看）

NT$80　NT$50

（聽）

Look at the picture.　How much is the hamburger?

　　A.　It's eighty dollars.

　　B.　It's fifty-five dollars.

　　C.　It's eighteen dollars.

正確答案為 A

Question 1

Question 2

Question 3

Question 4

Question 5

Question 6

請 翻 頁 ⬤⟹

Question 7

Question 8

Tom　Jack　David　John

Question 9

Question 10

請翻頁 ◖▭⟹

第二部份：問答

本部份共 10 題，每題錄音機會播出一個問句或直述句，每題播出一次，聽後請從試題冊上 A、B、C 三個選項中，選出一個最適合的回答或回應，並在答案紙上塗黑作答。

例：

（聽） Good morning, Kevin. How are you?

（看） A. I'm fine, thank you.
B. I'm in the living room.
C. My name is Kevin.

正確答案爲 A

11. A. It's going to be cloudy.
B. It's 34 degrees.
C. It's July 7th.

12. A. No, I've never met him.
B. Yes, I am.
C. No, I haven't.

13. A. Thank you.
B. I agree.
C. Of course not.

14. A. No. Mine is black.
B. Yes, this is yours.
C. I have a blue pen, too.

15. A. At six o'clock.
    B. I will.
    C. Don't worry. I won't.

16. A. Yes. Here it is.
    B. Yes, I do.
    C. Yes, I forgot.

17. A. I study seven subjects.
    B. I don't like history.
       It's too boring.
    C. Math. I always get
       good grades in that
       class.

18. A. There's one around
       the corner.
    B. It's on the shelf.
    C. Yes, I live over
       there.

19. A. Yes, I'll do it.
    B. Yes, I have it.
    C. No. It was too
       long.

20. A. She is nineteen.
    B. She's at the park.
    C. Her name is Eileen.

請 翻 頁 ⫸

第三部份： 簡短對話

　　本部份共 10 題，每題錄音機會播出一段對話及一個相關的問題，每題播出兩次，聽後請從試題冊上 A、B、C 三個選項中，選出一個最適合的回答，並在答案紙上塗黑作答。

例：

(聽) (Woman) Good afternoon, ...Mr. Davis?

　　　 (Man) 　　 Yes. I have an appointment with Dr. Sanders at two o'clock. My son Tommy has a fever.

　　　 (Woman) Oh, that's too bad. Well, please have a seat, Mr. Davis. Dr. Sanders will be right with you.

　　　 Question: Where did this conversation take place?

(看) A. In a post office.
　　 B. In a restaurant.
　　 C. In a doctor's office.

正確答案爲 C

21. A. She was sick.
　　B. Because she is better
　　　　now.
　　C. She was taking care
　　　　of her son.

22. A. He wants to call
　　　　someone who left
　　　　him a message.
　　B. He wants to call Sue,
　　　　but he cannot read
　　　　her phone number.
　　C. He wants to leave a
　　　　message.

23. A. She has visited
　　　　California twice.
　　B. She has never been
　　　　to California.
　　C. She has been to
　　　　Disneyland two
　　　　times.

24. A. He will buy a ticket
　　　　and stand on the
　　　　train.
　　B. He will wait for the
　　　　next train.
　　C. He will like standing
　　　　on the train.

25. A. She is confident
　　　　that she did well.
　　B. She is afraid that
　　　　she failed.
　　C. She hopes to get her
　　　　grade soon.

26. A. Keelung.
　　B. The same place the
　　　　woman is going.
　　C. Somewhere in the
　　　　south.

請 翻 頁 ▮⟹

27. A. She does not want to
       buy anything for the
       man.
    B. She is sorry she has
       to go shopping.
    C. She cannot buy fruit
       and vegetables.

28. A. That Joan wrote the
       man a letter.
    B. That Joan wrote a
       letter last week.
    C. That Joan's letter
       has not arrived.

29. A. The woman cannot
       have both vanilla
       and chocolate.
    B. The woman can
       have both vanilla
       and chocolate.
    C. The woman can
       have neither vanilla
       nor chocolate.

30. A. Confident.
    B. Worried.
    C. Excited.

初級英語聽力檢定 ② 詳解

第一部份

Look at the picture for question 1.

1. (**B**) Why is the man running?
   A. He is late for class.
   B. His train is going to leave soon.
   C. He is in a race.

   * run〔rʌn〕v. 跑　　race〔res〕n. 賽跑

Look at the picture for question 2.

2. (**C**) What is the boy dreaming?
   A. He is daydreaming.
   B. He is dreaming in bed.
   C. He is dreaming that he can fly.

   * dream〔drim〕v. 夢見
   daydream〔'de,drim〕v. 做白日夢　　fly〔flaɪ〕v. 飛

Look at the picture for question 3.

3. (**A**) What kind of movie is this?
   A. It is a western.
   B. It is a show on *Animal Planet*.
   C. It is a horror movie.

   * kind〔kaɪnd〕n. 種類　　western〔'wɛstɚn〕n. 西部片
   show〔ʃo〕n. 節目　　planet〔'plænɪt〕n. 行星
   Animal Planet 動物星球 (電視頻道名)
   horror〔'hɔrɚ〕adj. 恐怖的

Look at the picture for question 4.

4. (**C**) What is the man doing?

    A. He is eating lunch.

    B. He is cooking.

    C. He is eating bread.

    * cook〔kʊk〕v. 煮   bread〔brɛd〕n. 麵包

Look at the picture for question 5.

5. (**B**) How does the student feel?

    A. 100.

    B. Pleased.

    C. Embarrassed.

    * feel〔fil〕v. 感覺

    pleased〔plizd〕adj. 高興的

    embarrassed〔ɪmˈbærəst〕adj. 尷尬的

Look at the picture for question 6.

6. (**B**) What is the man's job?

    A. It is a gas station.

    B. Putting gas into cars.

    C. It is a gas pump.

    * job〔dʒɑb〕n. 工作

    gas〔gæs〕n. 汽油 (= *gasoline*)

    gas station 加油站   *put…into~* 把…灌入~

    pump〔pʌmp〕n. 幫浦;泵

    gas pump 汽油加油泵

Look at the picture for question 7.

7. (**B**) What is the woman doing?
    A. She is dreaming.
    B. She is talking to her boyfriend.
    C. She is talking to herself.

    * dream〔drim〕*v.* 作夢
    talk to ~　和～說話
    herself〔hɚ'sɛlf〕*pron.* 她自己

Look at the picture for question 8.

8. (**A**) Who is standing on the left side of Jack?
    A. Tom.
    B. David.
    C. John.

    * stand〔stænd〕*v.* 站
    on the left side of ~　在～的左邊

Look at the picture for question 9.

9. (**A**) Who is the woman talking to?
    A. Her granddaughter.
    B. Her husband.
    C. The telephone operator.

    * granddaughter〔'grænd,dɔtɚ〕*n.* 孫女
    husband〔'hʌzbənd〕*n.* 丈夫
    telephone〔'tɛlə,fon〕*n.* 電話
    operator〔'ɑpə,retɚ〕*n.* 接線生

Look at the picture for question 10.

10. (**B**) How does the first man in line feel?

    A. Bored.

    B. Angry.

    C. Patient.

    * **in line** 在隊伍中　　feel〔 fil 〕v. 覺得

    bored〔 bord 〕adj. 無聊的

    angry〔'æŋgrɪ〕adj. 生氣的

    patient〔'peʃənt〕adj. 有耐心的

第二部份

11. (**B**) What's the temperature today?

    A. It's going to be cloudy.

    B. It's 34 degrees.

    C. It's July 7th.

    * temperature〔'tɛmprətʃɚ〕n. 氣溫

    cloudy〔'klaʊdɪ〕adj. 多雲的　　degree〔 dɪ'gri 〕n. 度

    July〔 dʒu'laɪ 〕n. 七月

12. (**A**) Do you know Peter Lee?

    A. No, I've never met him.

    B. Yes, I am.

    C. No, I haven't.

    * never〔'nɛvɚ〕adv. 從未

    meet〔 mit 〕v. 和⋯見面；認識（三態變化為：meet-met-met）

13. (**B**) That was a terrible movie!

    A. Thank you.

    B. I agree.

    C. Of course not.

    * terrible〔'tɛrəbl̩〕 *adj.* 很糟的;可怕的

      agree〔ə'gri〕 *v.* 同意　　***of course*** 當然

14. (**A**) Is this your blue pen?

    A. No. Mine is black.

    B. Yes, this is yours.

    C. I have a blue pen, too.

    * ***blue pen*** 藍筆　　mine〔maɪn〕*pron.* 我的(東西)

15. (**B**) Please call me if you will be late.

    A. At six o'clock.

    B. I will.

    C. Don't worry. I won't.

    * call〔kɔl〕 *v.* 打電話給~　　worry〔'wɝɪ〕*v.* 擔心

16. (**A**) Did you remember the milk?

    A. Yes. Here it is.

    B. Yes, I do.

    C. Yes, I forgot.

    * remember〔rɪ'mɛmbɚ〕 *v.* 記得　　***Here it is.*** 在這裡。

      forget〔fɚ'gɛt〕 *v.* 忘記

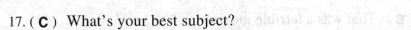

17. (**C**) What's your best subject?

    A. I study seven subjects.

    B. I don't like history. It's too boring.

    C. Math. I always get good grades in that class.

    * subject〔'sʌbdʒɪkt〕*n.* 科目　　history〔'hɪstrɪ〕*n.* 歷史

    boring〔'borɪŋ〕*adj.* 無聊的

    math〔mæθ〕*n.* 數學（= *mathematics*）

    grade〔gred〕*n.* 成績

18. (**A**) Is there a bank near here?

    A. There's one around the corner.

    B. It's on the shelf.

    C. Yes, I live over there.

    * bank〔bæŋk〕*n.* 銀行

    near〔nɪr〕*prep.* 在…附近

    around〔ə'raʊnd〕*prep.* 在…附近

    corner〔'kɔrnɚ〕*n.* 轉角

    shelf〔ʃɛlf〕*n.* 架子　　***over there*** 在那邊

19. (**C**) Did you finish reading chapter 17?

    A. Yes, I'll do it.

    B. Yes, I have it.

    C. No. It was too long.

    * finish〔'fɪnɪʃ〕*v.* 完成

    chapter〔'tʃæptɚ〕*n.* 章節

    long〔lɔŋ〕*adj.* 長的

20. (**B**) Where is your sister?

A. She is nineteen.

B. She's at the park.

C. Her name is Eileen.

* nineteen〔'naɪn'tin〕*adj.* 十九歲的

park〔pɑrk〕*n.* 公園 name〔nem〕*n.* 名字

Eileen〔'aɪlin〕*n.* 艾琳（女子名）

第三部份

21. (**C**) M：Where were you yesterday?

W：My son was sick so I took a day off.

M：Oh, is he better now?

W：Yes, thanks.

Question：Why didn't the man see the woman yesterday?

A. She was sick.

B. Because she is better now.

C. She was taking care of her son.

* son〔sʌn〕*n.* 兒子 sick〔sɪk〕*adj.* 生病的

take a day off 請一天假

better〔'bɛtɚ〕*adj.*（病痛）有好轉

take care of 照顧

22. (**A**) M：Can you read the phone number on this message?

W：No, it's not clear enough.

M：I'll ask Sue.　I think she took the message.

Question：What does the man want to do?

A. He wants to call someone who left him a message.

B. He wants to call Sue, but he cannot read her phone number.

C. He wants to leave a message.

* read〔rid〕*v.* 看懂　　*phone number* 電話號碼
message〔'mɛsɪdʒ〕*n.* 信息；留言
clear〔klɪr〕*adj.* 清楚的　　think〔θɪŋk〕*v.* 認為
take〔tek〕*v.* 記下　　leave〔liv〕*v.* 留給；留下

23. (**C**) M：What is your favorite place in California?

W：I like Disneyland best.

M：How many times have you been there?

W：Twice.

Question：What did the woman say?

A. She has visited California twice.

B. She has never been to California.

C. She has been to Disneyland two times.

* favorite〔'fevərɪt〕*adj.* 最喜愛的
California〔,kælə'fɔrnjə〕*n.* 加州
Disneyland〔'dɪznɪ,lænd〕*n.* 迪士尼樂園
like…best 最喜歡…　　time〔taɪm〕*n.* 次數
twice〔twaɪs〕*adv.* 兩次　　visit〔'vɪzɪt〕*v.* 拜訪；遊覽
have never been to 從未去過

24. (**A**) M：Are there any seats left on the 6:30 train?

W：No, there aren't any seats.　But you can stand if you like.

M：I guess I'll have to.

Question：What will the man do?

A. He will buy a ticket and stand on the train.

B. He will wait for the next train.

C. He will like standing on the train.

* seat〔sit〕*n.* 座位　　left〔lɛft〕*adj.* 剩下的
  if you like 如果你願意的話　　guess〔gɛs〕*v.* 猜想；認爲
  have to 必須　　ticket〔'tɪkɪt〕*n.* 車票

25. (**B**) M：How did you do on the test?

W：I don't know.　We haven't gotten our grades yet.

M：Do you think you passed?

W：I hope so, but I'm not too confident.

Question：How does the woman think she did on the test?

A. She is confident that she did well.

B. She is afraid that she failed.

C. She hopes to get her grade soon.

* ***How did you do on the test?*** 你考試考得如何？
  grade〔gred〕*n.* 成績　　***not…yet*** 尚未
  pass〔pæs〕*v.*（考試）及格　　hope〔hop〕*v.* 希望
  so〔so〕*adv.* 如此　　confident〔'kɑnfədnt〕*adj.* 有信心的
  do well 考得好　　afraid〔ə'fred〕*adj.* 害怕的；擔心的
  fail〔fel〕*v.*（考試）不及格
  soon〔sun〕*adv.* 馬上；很快地

26. (**C**) M：Excuse me, where is this train going?

W：It's northbound. It's going to Keelung.

M：Oh! I need to go to the other platform!

Question：Where is the man probably going?

A. Keelung.

B. The same place the woman is going.

C. Somewhere in the south.

* train〔tren〕*n.* 火車
  northbound〔'nɔrθ,baʊnd〕*adj.* 北行的
  Keelung〔'ki'lʌŋ〕*n.* 基隆
  platform〔'plæt,fɔrm〕*n.* 月台
  probably〔'prɑbəblɪ〕*adv.* 可能
  same〔sem〕*adj.* 相同的
  somewhere〔'sʌm,wɛr〕*adv.* 某處
  south〔saʊθ〕*n.* 南方

27. (**C**) M：Are you going shopping?

W：Yes. Do you need something?

M：Could you buy some fruit and vegetables for me?

W：I'm sorry, but I'm going to 7-Eleven.

Question：What does the woman mean?

A. She does not want to buy anything for the man.

B. She is sorry she has to go shopping.

C. She cannot buy fruit and vegetables.

* ***go shopping*** 去購物　　need〔nid〕*v.* 需要
  fruit〔frut〕*n.* 水果　　vegetable〔'vɛdʒətəbḷ〕*n.* 蔬菜
  mean〔min〕*v.* 意思是

28. (**C**) M：Has the mailman come yet?

W：Yes, but there is no mail for you.

M：That's strange. Joan said she sent me a letter last week.

Question：What is strange?

A. That Joan wrote the man a letter.

B. That Joan wrote a letter last week.

C. That Joan's letter has not arrived.

* mailman〔'mel,mæn〕*n.* 郵差
yet〔jɛt〕*adv.* 已經（用於疑問句）
mail〔mel〕*n.* 信件　strange〔strendʒ〕*adj.* 奇怪的
send〔sɛnd〕*v.* 寄　arrive〔ə'raɪv〕*v.* 抵達

29. (**B**) M：What kind of ice cream would you like?

W：I can't decide. I like both vanilla and chocolate.

M：Why not have both?

Question：What does the man mean?

A. The woman cannot have both vanilla and chocolate.

B. The woman can have both vanilla and chocolate.

C. The woman can have neither vanilla nor chocolate.

* *ice cream* 冰淇淋　decide〔dɪ'saɪd〕*v.* 決定
vanilla〔və'nɪlə〕*adj.* 香草的
chocolate〔'tʃɔkəlɪt〕*adj.* 巧克力的
Why not V. ~ ? 爲何不~ ?
neither…nor ~ 旣不…也不~

30. (**B**) M：What day is your concert?

W：It's on Wednesday.

M：Are you excited?

W：No. I'm nervous. I need to practice more.

Question：How does the woman feel?

A. Confident.

B. Worried.

C. Excited.

* concert〔'kɑnsɜt〕 *n.* 音樂會

　Wednesday〔'wɛnzdɪ, -de〕 *n.* 星期三

　excited〔 ɪk'saɪtɪd〕 *adj.* 興奮的

　nervous〔'nɜvəs〕 *adj.* 緊張的

　practice〔'præktɪs〕 *v.* 練習

　confident〔'kɑnfədənt〕 *adj.* 有信心的

　worried〔'wɜɪd〕 *adj.* 擔心的

全民英語能力分級檢定測驗
初級測驗③

　　本測驗分三部份，全為三選一之選擇題，每部份各 10 題，共 30 題，作答時間約 20 分鐘。

第一部份：看圖辨義

　　　　本部份共 10 題，試題冊上每題有一個圖片，請聽錄音機播出一個相關的問題，與 A、B、C 三個英語敘述後，選一個與所看到圖片最相符的答案，並在答案紙上相對的圓圈內塗黑作答。每題播出一遍，問題及選項均不印在試題冊上。

例：(看)

NT$80　NT$50

(聽)

Look at the picture.　How much is the hamburger?

　　A.　It's eighty dollars.
　　B.　It's fifty-five dollars.
　　C.　It's eighteen dollars.

正確答案為 A

Question 1

Question 2

Question 3

Question 4

Question 5

Question 6

請翻頁 ▯⟹

Question 7

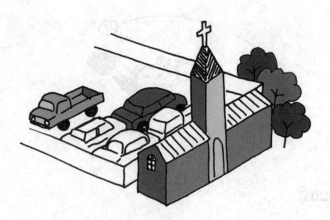

Question 8

Question 9

Question 10

請翻頁 ▮▭▭⟹

第二部份： 問答

本部份共 10 題，每題錄音機會播出一個問句或直述句，
每題播出一次，聽後請從試題冊上 A、B、C 三個選項
中，選出一個最適合的回答或回應，並在答案紙上塗黑
作答。

例：

（聽） Good morning, Kevin. How are you?

（看） A. I'm fine, thank you.
　　　 B. I'm in the living room.
　　　 C. My name is Kevin.

正確答案爲 A

11. A. Two times two is
　　　　four.
　　B. It's four-thirty.
　　C. No, I haven't.

12. A. At age 16.
　　B. I will be a teacher.
　　C. In Taichung.

13. A. It's at four o'clock.
　　B. In the refrigerator.
　　C. I have a headache.

14. A. I'm not on the team.
　　B. Yes, it's my favorite
　　　　sport.
　　C. No, I don't know how.

15. A. The one wearing a
　　　blue dress.
　　B. She is 12 years old.
　　C. She likes to play the
　　　piano.

16. A. By bicycle.
　　B. In the afternoon.
　　C. About a kilometer.

17. A. Yes, I do.
　　B. Funny ones.
　　C. I've already seen it.

18. A. That will be ten
　　　dollars, please.
　　B. Thanks for returning
　　　it.
　　C. Of course you can.

19. A. I usually have eggs.
　　B. At six o'clock.
　　C. I always eat out.

20. A. I hope I will.
　　B. It was okay.
　　C. Just study hard.

請 翻 頁 ⬅➡

第三部份：　簡短對話

　　　　　本部份共 10 題，每題錄音機會播出一段對話及一個相關
　　　　　的問題，每題播出兩次，聽後請從試題冊上 A、B、C 三
　　　　　個選項中，選出一個最適合的回答，並在答案紙上塗黑
　　　　　作答。

　　　例：

　　（聽）(Woman)　Good afternoon, …Mr. Davis?

　　　　　(Man)　　Yes.　I have an appointment with
　　　　　　　　　　Dr. Sanders at two o'clock.　My
　　　　　　　　　　son Tommy has a fever.

　　　　　(Woman)　Oh, that's too bad.　Well, please
　　　　　　　　　　have a seat, Mr. Davis.　Dr.
　　　　　　　　　　Sanders will be right with you.

　　　　　Question:　Where did this conversation take
　　　　　　　　　　place?

　　（看）A.　In a post office.
　　　　　B.　In a restaurant.
　　　　　C.　In a doctor's office.

　　　　　正確答案為 C

21. A. He ate the woman's
　　 chocolate cake.
　 B. He ordered a
　　 cheesecake.
　 C. He brought the
　　 wrong cake.

22. A. She will drive the
　　 man to the party.
　 B. She wants the man
　　 to come to her party.
　 C. She will give the
　　 man a car.

23. A. She thinks the snow
　　 is beautiful.
　 B. She doesn't like it.
　 C. She likes to feel cold.

24. A. Her parents won't
　　 allow it.
　 B. It is quiet.
　 C. It is boring.

25. A. The vase is too old.
　 B. The vase is not very
　　 pretty.
　 C. The vase costs a lot
　　 of money.

26. A. Help the woman
　　 find the restaurant.
　 B. Ask someone where
　　 the theater is.
　 C. Ask the woman for
　　 help.

請 翻 頁 ⮕

27. A. She often goes to
       Kenting.
    B. She lives in Kenting.
    C. She has ten friends
       in Kenting.

28. A. Start the concert a
       half hour early.
    B. Leave for the concert
       30 minutes before it
       starts.
    C. Arrive at the concert
       at 6:30.

29. A. It belongs to the
       woman.
    B. It is not green.
    C. The woman doesn't
       know the man.

30. A. She got contact
       lenses.
    B. She lost her glasses.
    C. She left her glasses
       on the bus.

初級英語聽力檢定③詳解

第一部份

Look at the picture for question 1.

1. (**A**) What is the man doing to the car?

  A. He is trying to fix it.

  B. He is washing it.

  C. Because he does not know how.

  * try〔traɪ〕*v.* 設法；嘗試 fix〔fɪks〕*v.* 修理
  wash〔wɑʃ〕*v.* 清洗 because〔bɪˈkɔz〕*conj.* 因為

Look at the picture for question 2.

2. (**C**) Where is the boy?

  A. He is her grandson.

  B. It is a picture.

  C. The woman does not know.

  * grandson〔ˈgrænd͵sʌn〕*n.* 孫子
  picture〔ˈpɪktʃ⊕〕*n.* 照片

Look at the picture for question 3.

3. (**C**) What is happening?

  A. No, it is not happy.

  B. The cat likes the dog.

  C. The dog is chasing the cat.

  * happen〔ˈhæpən〕*v.* 發生 chase〔tʃes〕*v.* 追逐

Look at the picture for question 4.

4. (**B**) What sport is he playing?

    A. He is catching the ball.

    B. It is baseball.

    C. He will miss it.

    * sport〔sport〕*n.* 運動　　play〔ple〕*v.* 做（運動）

      catch〔kætʃ〕*v.* 接住　　baseball〔'bes,bɔl〕*n.* 棒球

      miss〔mɪs〕*v.* 錯過；未接到

Look at the picture for question 5.

5. (**B**) What is the girl doing?

    A. She received a letter.

    B. She is writing to her grandfather.

    C. She will mail it.

    * receive〔rɪ'siv〕*v.* 收到　　***write to*** ～ 寫信給～

      grandfather〔'grænd,faðɚ〕*n.* 爺爺

      mail〔mel〕*v.* 郵寄

Look at the picture for question 6.

6. (**C**) How are they washing the dishes?

    A. There are too many.

    B. Two people.

    C. Very quickly.

    * dish〔dɪʃ〕*n.* 碗盤　　quickly〔'kwɪklɪ〕*adv.* 快地

Look at the picture for question 7.

7. (**C**) Where are the cars?

  A. They are in the church.

  B. It is a parking lot.

  C. They are behind the church.

   * church〔tʃɝtʃ〕*n.* 教堂   ***parking lot*** 停車場
   behind〔bɪˈhaɪnd〕*prep.* 在⋯後面

Look at the picture for question 8.

8. (**A**) What is in front of the shop?

  A. It is a bus stop.

  B. It is a flower shop.

  C. It is a window.

   * ***in front of*** ⋯ 在⋯前面   shop〔ʃɑp〕*n.* 商店
   bus stop 公車站   ***flower shop*** 花店
   window〔ˈwɪndo〕*n.* 窗戶；（商店）櫥窗

Look at the picture for question 9.

9. (**C**) Why is he crying?

  A. He lost his homework.

  B. The boy is crying.

  C. His father is angry.

   * cry〔kraɪ〕*v.* 哭
   lose〔luz〕*v.* 遺失（三態變化為：lose-lost-lost）
   homework〔ˈhom,wɝk〕*n.* 家庭作業
   angry〔ˈæŋgrɪ〕*adj.* 生氣的

Look at the picture for question 10.

10. (**B**) Who is the man?

    A. He hurried to catch the train.

    B. He is a passenger.

    C. He was running.

    * hurry〔'hɜɪ〕v. 匆忙　　catch〔kætʃ〕v. 趕上

    train〔tren〕n. 火車

    passenger〔'pæsṇdʒɚ〕n. 乘客

    run〔rʌn〕v. 跑

第二部份

11. (**B**) Do you know the time?

    A. Two times two is four.

    B. It's four-thirty.

    C. No, I haven't.

    * *the time* 幾點幾分；時刻

    time〔taɪm〕*prep.* 乘　　*four-thirty* 四點三十分

12. (**C**) Where did you grow up?

    A. At age 16.

    B. I will be a teacher.

    C. In Taichung.

    * *grow up* 長大　　age〔edʒ〕n. 年齡

    Taichung〔'taɪ'tʃuŋ〕n. 台中

13. (**C**) What's the matter?

　　　A. It's at four o'clock.

　　　B. In the refrigerator.

　　　C. I have a headache.

　　　* **What's the matter?** 怎麼了？
　　　refrigerator〔rɪ'frɪdʒə,retə〕n. 冰箱
　　　headache〔'hɛd,ek〕n. 頭痛

14. (**B**) Do you like to watch basketball?

　　　A. I'm not on the team.

　　　B. Yes, it's my favorite sport.

　　　C. No, I don't know how.

　　　* basketball〔'bæskɪt,bɔl〕n. 籃球
　　　team〔tim〕n. 隊；組
　　　favorite〔'fevərɪt〕adj. 最喜愛的
　　　sport〔sport〕n. 運動

15. (**A**) Which girl is your cousin?

　　　A. The one wearing a blue dress.

　　　B. She is 12 years old.

　　　C. She likes to play the piano.

　　　* cousin〔'kʌzn̩〕n. 表（堂）兄弟姊妹
　　　wear〔wɛr〕v. 穿著　　dress〔drɛs〕n. 洋裝
　　　piano〔pɪ'æno〕n. 鋼琴

16. (**C**) How far is the park from here?
　　A. By bicycle.
　　B. In the afternoon.
　　C. About a kilometer.

　　* **How far ~?** ～多遠? 　kilometer〔ˈkɪləˌmɪtɚ〕n. 公里

17. (**B**) What kind of movies do you like?
　　A. Yes, I do.
　　B. Funny ones.
　　C. I've already seen it.

　　* kind〔kaɪnd〕n. 種類　funny〔ˈfʌnɪ〕adj. 好笑的
　　already〔ɔlˈrɛdɪ〕adv. 已經

18. (**B**) Here is that book I borrowed from you.
　　A. That will be ten dollars, please.
　　B. Thanks for returning it.
　　C. Of course you can.

　　* borrow〔ˈbaro〕v. 借 (入)
　　return〔rɪˈtɝn〕v. 歸還　**of course** 當然

19. (**C**) Who makes your breakfast?
　　A. I usually have eggs.
　　B. At six o'clock.
　　C. I always eat out.

　　* make〔mek〕v. 做;準備
　　breakfast〔ˈbrɛkfəst〕n. 早餐　have〔hæv〕v. 吃
　　egg〔ɛg〕n. 蛋　**eat out** 在外面吃

20. (**B**) Did you get a good grade on that exam?

    A. I hope I will.

    B. It was okay.

    C. Just study hard.

    * grade〔gred〕*n.* 成績

       exam〔ɪg'zæm〕*n.* 考試   hope〔hop〕*v.* 希望

       okay〔'o'ke〕*adj.* 沒問題的（= *OK* ）

       hard〔hɑrd〕*adv.* 努力地

第三部份

21. (**C**) M：Here is the cheesecake you ordered.

    W：I didn't order cheesecake. I want chocolate cake.

    M：Oh, sorry.

    Question：What did the man do?

    A. He ate the woman's chocolate cake.

    B. He ordered a cheesecake.

    C. He brought the wrong cake.

    * cheesecake〔'tʃiz,kek〕*n.* 起司蛋糕

       order〔'ɔrdɚ〕*v.* 點（菜）

       chocolate〔'tʃɔkəlɪt〕*adj.* 巧克力的

       bring〔brɪŋ〕*v.* 帶來

       wrong〔rɔŋ〕*adj.* 錯誤的

22. (**A**) M: Are you going to Jack's party?

W: Of course. Are you?

M: I want to, but I don't have a car.

W: No problem. You can come with me.

Question: What does the woman mean?

A. She will drive the man to the party.

B. She wants the man to come to her party.

C. She will give the man a car.

* ***no problem*** 沒問題

mean〔min〕v. 意思是

drive〔draɪv〕v. 開車載 (人)

23. (**B**) M: What's the weather like in winter in your
hometown?

W: Oh, it's very cold and there is a lot of snow.

M: Do you play in the snow?

W: No. I don't like cold weather.

Question: How does the woman feel about the winter
weather in her hometown?

A. She thinks the snow is beautiful.

B. She doesn't like it.

C. She likes to feel cold.

* ***What's～like?*** ～怎麼樣? weather〔'wɛðɚ〕n. 天氣

winter〔'wɪntɚ〕n. 冬天

hometown〔'hom'taʊn〕n. 家鄉 feel〔fil〕v. 覺得

24.(**B**) M：Do you have any pets?

W：No, but my sister has a goldfish.

M：Is that all? Fish are a little boring.

W：Yes. But my parents won't allow us to have a noisy pet.

Question：Why does the woman's sister have a pet goldfish?

A. Her parents won't allow it.

B. It is quiet.　　　　C. It is boring.

* pet〔pɛt〕*n.* 寵物　*adj.*（作）寵物的
goldfish〔'gold,fıʃ〕*n.* 金魚　　***Is that all?*** 就這樣？
boring〔'borıŋ〕*adj.* 無聊的　　allow〔ə'laʊ〕*v.* 允許
noisy〔'nɔızı〕*adj.* 吵鬧的　　quiet〔'kwaıət〕*adj.* 安靜的

25.(**C**) M：Why is this vase so expensive?

W：It is very old.

M：It's beautiful, but I don't have enough money. Can you give me a discount?

W：No, I'm sorry but I can't.

Question：Why does the man ask for a discount?

A. The vase is too old.

B. The vase is not very pretty.

C. The vase costs a lot of money.

* vase〔ves〕*n.* 花瓶　expensive〔ık'spɛnsıv〕*adj.* 昂貴的
discount〔'dıskaʊnt〕*n.* 折扣　***ask for*** ~ 請求~
pretty〔'prıtı〕*adj.* 漂亮的　cost〔kɔst〕*v.* 值…（錢）
a lot of 許多的

26. (**B**) M : Do you know where the theater is?

W : No, I don't.

M : Maybe we should ask for help.

Question : What does the man want to do?

A. Help the woman find the restaurant.

B. Ask someone where the theater is.

C. Ask the woman for help.

* theater ('θiətə) *n.* 戲院　　maybe ('mebi) *adv.* 也許

help (hɛlp) *n.* 幫助　　find (faɪnd) *v.* 找到

restaurant ('rɛstərənt) *n.* 餐廳

ask sb. for help 請某人幫忙

27. (**A**) M : How many times have you been to Kenting?

W : At least ten times.

M : You must like it a lot.

W : Oh, yes! I wish I could live there.

Question : What is true about the woman?

A. She often goes to Kenting.

B. She lives in Kenting.

C. She has ten friends in Kenting.

* time (taɪm) *n.* 次數　　Kenting ('kɛn'tɪŋ) *n.* 墾丁

at least 至少　　***a lot*** 非常地 (表程度)

wish (wɪʃ) *v.* 但願　　true (tru) *adj.* 真的

often ('ɔfən) *adv.* 經常

28. (**C**) M：What time does the concert start?

W：At seven, but we should go there early to get good seats.

M：OK. Let's arrive a half hour before it starts.

Question：What will they do?

A. Start the concert a half hour early.

B. Leave for the concert 30 minutes before it starts.

C. Arrive at the concert at 6:30.

* concert〔'kɑnsɜt〕*n.* 音樂會　　start〔stɑrt〕*v.* 開始
get〔gɛt〕*v.* 得到　　seat〔sit〕*n.* 座位
arrive〔ə'raɪv〕*v.* 抵達　　*a half hour* 半個小時
early〔'ɜlɪ〕*adv.* (比預定的時間) 早
leave for 動身前往

29. (**B**) M：Isn't that your jacket on the chair?

W：No. My jacket is green.

M：Then whose is that?

W：I don't know.

Question：What do we know about the jacket?

A. It belongs to the woman.

B. It is not green.

C. The woman doesn't know the man.

* jacket〔'dʒækɪt〕*n.* 夾克　　chair〔tʃɛr〕*n.* 椅子
green〔grin〕*adj.* 綠的　　know〔no〕*v.* 知道；認識
belong〔bə'lɔŋ〕*v.* 屬於

30. (**A**) M：Wow! You look so different without your glasses!

W：Thanks. It's really convenient, too.

M：How long can you leave them in your eyes?

W：All day.

Question：What did the woman do?

A. She got contact lenses.

B. She lost her glasses.

C. She left her glasses on the bus.

* wow〔waʊ〕*interj.* 哇！（驚訝時所發出的感歎）

different〔ˈdɪfərənt〕*adj.* 不同的

without〔wɪðˈaʊt〕*prep.* 沒有

glasses〔ˈglæsɪz〕*n. pl.* 眼鏡

convenient〔kənˈvinjənt〕*adj.* 方便的

How long ～? ～多久？

leave〔liv〕*v.* 使處於（某種狀態）；遺留

get〔gɛt〕*v.* 買　　contact〔ˈkɑntækt〕*adj.* 接觸的

lenses〔lɛnzɪz〕*n. pl.* 鏡片　　***contact lenses*** 隱形眼鏡

lose〔luz〕*v.* 遺失

全民英語能力分級檢定測驗

初級測驗④

本測驗分三部份，全為三選一之選擇題，每部份各 10 題，共 30 題，作答時間約 20 分鐘。

第一部份：看圖辨義

本部份共 10 題，試題冊上每題有一個圖片，請聽錄音機播出一個相關的問題，與 A、B、C 三個英語敘述後，選一個與所看到圖片最相符的答案，並在答案紙上相對的圓圈內塗黑作答。每題播出一遍，問題及選項均不印在試題冊上。

例：（看）

NT$80　NT$50

（聽）

Look at the picture.　How much is the hamburger?

  A.　It's eighty dollars.

  B.　It's fifty-five dollars.

  C.　It's eighteen dollars.

正確答案為 A

Question 1

Question 2

Question 3

Question 4

請 翻 頁 ⮕

Question 5

Question 6

Question 7

Question 8

Question 9

Question 10

請 翻 頁 ◪⟹

第二部份： 問答

　　　本部份共 10 題，每題錄音機會播出一個問句或直述句，
　　　每題播出一次，聽後請從試題冊上 A、B、C 三個選項
　　　中，選出一個最適合的回答或回應，並在答案紙上塗黑
　　　作答。

例：

　（聽）　Good morning, Kevin. How are you?

　（看）　A.　I'm fine, thank you.
　　　　　B.　I'm in the living room.
　　　　　C.　My name is Kevin.

　　　　　正確答案為 A

11. A. I'll be here at 3:00.

　　B. Thank you, nurse.

　　C. Don't mention it, doctor.

12. A. I was talking to my sister.

　　B. I'm sorry, but I'm too busy.

　　C. Phone me when you're not busy.

13. A. The new book will go on sale soon.

　　B. Oh, I've read them all.

　　C. They are in the library.

14. A. Yes, I will.

　　B. No, I don't.

　　C. No, I didn't.

15. A. Thank you, I will.
    B. I can't help it.
    C. You're welcome.

16. A. I bought two shirts.
    B. Yes. We went
       shopping together.
    C. Yes, she does.

17. A. About five minutes
       ago.
    B. I came to see John.
    C. I came by taxi.

18. A. Yes, I can.
    B. No, I don't.
    C. Of course I am.

19. A. Thank you. Here is
       mine.
    B. Thanks. Same to you.
    C. Thanks, but I can't
       open it.

20. A. Yes, you may.
    B. Yes, I drank them.
    C. I like both.

請 翻 頁 ⇒

第三部份： 簡短對話

本部份共 10 題，每題錄音機會播出一段對話及一個相關
的問題，每題播出兩次，聽後請從試題冊上 A、B、C 三
個選項中，選出一個最適合的回答，並在答案紙上塗黑
作答。

例：

（聽）	(Woman)	Good afternoon, …Mr. Davis?
	(Man)	Yes. I have an appointment with Dr. Sanders at two o'clock. My son Tommy has a fever.
	(Woman)	Oh, that's too bad. Well, please have a seat, Mr. Davis. Dr. Sanders will be right with you.
	Question:	Where did this conversation take place?

（看） A. In a post office.
　　　B. In a restaurant.
　　　C. In a doctor's office.

正確答案爲 C

21. A. The woman should
　　 give up her lessons.
　　B. The woman should
　　 continue her
　　 lessons.
　　C. He would like to
　　 give the woman
　　 violin lessons.

22. A. The girl did not get
　　 to school on time.
　　B. There was a serious
　　 traffic jam.
　　C. She is usually the
　　 first one to arrive at
　　 school.

23. A. It is a good place to
　　 eat dinner.
　　B. They need energy
　　 for bowling.
　　C. It is Joan's birthday.

24. A. In a car.
　　B. On an airplane.
　　C. On a boat.

25. A. She is a fan of Brad
　　 Pitt.
　　B. She is taking care of
　　 Brad Pitt's cat.
　　C. Her cat looks like
　　 Brad Pitt's cat.

請 翻 頁 ⫸

26. A. She will write an
   important letter.
   B. She will go to the post
   office right away.
   C. She will ask the man to
   do it right now.

27. A. Hamburgers should be
   eaten only at lunchtime.
   B. He does not like
   hamburgers.
   C. He doesn't want to eat
   two hamburgers in one
   day.

28. A. The woman should see
   a doctor right away.
   B. The woman will feel
   better tomorrow.
   C. The woman should rest.

29. A. He will try on a
   different jacket.
   B. He will try to find
   a jacket in a
   different store.
   C. He will try to get
   a discount.

30. A. It is a police car.
   B. The police told
   her to move it.
   C. Parking is not
   allowed in front
   of the building.

初級英語聽力檢定④詳解

第一部份

Look at the picture for question 1.

1. (**C**) How is the weather?

    A. It is delicious.   B. It is nice and cold.

    C. It is hot and sunny.

    * weather〔ˈwɛðɚ〕*n.* 天氣

      delicious〔dɪˈlɪʃəs〕*adj.* 美味的

      nice and 非常；挺（口語用法，放在形容詞前）

      sunny〔ˈsʌnɪ〕*adj.* 陽光普照的；晴朗的

Look at the picture for question 2.

2. (**B**) What is the girl on the right doing?

    A. She is scared.

    B. She is telling ghost stories.

    C. She is sleeping.

    * right〔raɪt〕*n.* 右邊   scared〔skɛrd〕*adj.* 怕害的

      ghost〔gost〕*n.* 鬼

Look at the picture for question 3.

3. (**B**) Is the man sleeping?

    A. Yes, he is in bed.   B. No. It is too noisy.

    C. Because he is tired.

    * ***be in bed*** 躺臥床上   noisy〔ˈnɔɪzɪ〕*adj.* 吵鬧的

      tired〔taɪrd〕*adj.* 疲倦的

Look at the picture for question 4.

4. (**A**) What season is it?

    A. It is autumn.

    B. They are falling.

    C. It is a forest.

    * season〔'sizn〕*n.* 季節　　autumn〔'ɔtəm〕*n.* 秋天

    fall〔fɔl〕*v.* 掉落　*n.* 秋天

    forest〔'fɔrɪst〕*n.* 森林

Look at the picture for question 5.

5. (**C**) What will the man next to the tree do?

    A. He is yelling for help.

    B. He cannot swim.

    C. He will throw a rope.

    * *next to* ～　在～旁邊　　yell〔jɛl〕*v.* 大叫

    swim〔swɪm〕*v.* 游泳　　throw〔θro〕*v.* 丟

    rope〔rop〕*n.* 繩子

Look at the picture for question 6.

6. (**C**) Where is the man going?

    A. A glass of water.

    B. In a desert.

    C. To the trees.

    * *a glass of* ～　一杯～

    desert〔'dɛzət〕*n.* 沙漠

Look at the picture for question 7.

7. (**B**) Where has the woman been?

      A. She enjoys shopping.

      B. She has been to the market.

      C. She is going home.

      * enjoy〔ɪn'dʒɔɪ〕*v.* 喜歡   shop〔ʃɑp〕*v.* 購物

      have been to ~ 曾去過~

      market〔'mɑrkɪt〕*n.* 市場

Look at the picture for question 8.

8. (**C**) What is he reading?

      A. A novel.

      B. He is hiking.

      C. A map.

      * novel〔'nɑvḷ〕*n.* 小說

      hike〔haɪk〕*v.* 健行；徒步旅行

      map〔mæp〕*n.* 地圖

Look at the picture for question 9.

9. (**A**) What is cooking?

      A. It is beef.

      B. It is oven.

      C. On the fire.

      * cook〔kʊk〕*v.* (食物)在煮著   beef〔bif〕*n.* 牛肉

      oven〔'ʌvən〕*n.* 爐子；烤箱   fire〔faɪr〕*n.* 火；爐火

Look at the picture for question 10.

10. (**B**) What is the man on the left doing?

　　　A. He is talking.

　　　B. He is holding a suitcase.

　　　C. He is writing his name.

　　　* left〔lɛft〕n. 左邊　　hold〔hold〕v. 拿著；提著
　　　　suitcase〔'sut,kes〕n. 手提箱　　write〔raɪt〕v. 寫

第二部份

11. (**B**) I'll tell the doctor that you're here.

　　　A. I'll be here at 3:00.

　　　B. Thank you, nurse.

　　　C. Don't mention it, doctor.

　　　* doctor〔'dɑktɚ〕n. 醫生　　nurse〔nɝs〕n. 護士
　　　　mention〔'mɛnʃən〕v. 提起（事）
　　　　Don't mention it. 不客氣。

12. (**A**) I tried to call you but your phone was busy.

　　　A. I was talking to my sister.

　　　B. I'm sorry, but I'm too busy.

　　　C. Phone me when you're not busy.

　　　* try〔traɪ〕v. 嘗試；想要
　　　　call〔kɔl〕v. 打電話給～
　　　　phone〔fon〕n. 電話　　v. 打電話給～（ = *telephone* ）
　　　　busy〔'bɪzɪ〕adj.（電話）忙線中；忙碌的

13. (**B**) How many *Harry Potter* books have you read?

    A. The new book will go on sale soon.

    B. Oh, I've read them all.

    C. They are in the library.

    * ***Harry Potter*** 哈利波特（小説名）

    on sale 上市銷售；特價出售

    soon〔sun〕*adv.* 不久；很快地

    library〔'laɪˌbrɛrɪ〕*n.* 圖書館

14. (**C**) Did you walk the dog?

    A. Yes, I will.

    B. No, I don't.

    C. No, I didn't.

    * walk〔wɔk〕*v.* 遛（狗等）

15. (**A**) Help yourself to some tea.

    A. Thank you, I will.

    B. I can't help it.

    C. You're welcome.

    * ***help*** *oneself* ***to*** 隨意取用（食物等）

    help〔hɛlp〕*v.* 避免

    cannot help ***V.*** 不得不；忍不住

    I can't help it. 我忍不住；我沒辦法。

    You're welcome. 不客氣。

16. (**B**) Did you see Karen at the mall?

    A. I bought two shirts.

    B. Yes. We went shopping together.

    C. Yes, she does.

    * mall〔mɔl〕*n.* 購物中心

    buy〔baɪ〕*v.* 買（三態變化爲：buy-bought〔bɔt〕-bought）

    shirt〔ʃɜt〕*n.* 襯衫   shop〔ʃɑp〕*v.* 購物

    go shopping 去購物   together〔tə'gɛðɚ〕*adv.* 一起

17. (**C**) How did you get here?

    A. About five minutes ago.

    B. I came to see John.

    C. I came by taxi.

    * get〔gɛt〕*v.* 抵達   by〔baɪ〕*prep.* 搭乘（交通工具）

18. (**B**) Do you know how to drive?

    A. Yes, I can.   B. No, I don't.

    C. Of course I am.

    * drive〔draɪv〕*v.* 開車   ***of course*** 當然

19. (**A**) Here is my email address.

    A. Thank you. Here is mine.

    B. Thanks. Same to you.

    C. Thanks, but I can't open it.

    * ***Here is ~ .*** 這是～。 email〔'i‚mel〕*n.* 電子郵件 (= *e-mail*)

    address〔ə'drɛs, 'ædrɛs〕*n.* 地址

    mine〔maɪn〕*pron.* 我的（東西）

    Same to you. 你也一樣。（回應別人的祝福）

20. (**C**) Do you drink coffee or tea?

    A. Yes, you may.

    B. Yes, I drank them.

    C. I like both.

    * drink〔drɪŋk〕v. 喝（三態變化為：drink-drank-drunk）

     coffee〔'kɔfɪ〕n. 咖啡 both〔boθ〕pron. 兩者

第三部份

21. (**B**) M：Can you play an instrument?

    W：I took violin lessons last year, but I wasn't

      very good.

    M：You shouldn't give up. I'm sure you can do it.

    Question：What does the man mean?

    A. The woman should give up her lessons.

    B. The woman should continue her lessons.

    C. He would like to give the woman violin lessons.

    * play〔ple〕v. 演奏

     instrument〔'ɪnstrəmənt〕n. 樂器

     take〔tek〕v. 上（課）

     violin〔,vaɪə'lɪn〕n. 小提琴 lesson〔'lɛsn̩〕n. 課程

     give up 放棄 sure〔ʃur〕adj. 確信的

     continue〔kən'tɪnju〕v. 繼續

     would like to V. 想要～（= *want to V.*）

     give〔gɪv〕v. 講（課）

22. (**A**) M：Were you late for school today?

W：Yes. But how did you know?

M：Your teacher called me.

W：Well, it wasn't my fault. There was a traffic jam. Besides, it's the first time I've ever been late.

Question：Why did the girl's teacher call her father?

A. The girl did not get to school on time.

B. There was a serious traffic jam.

C. She is usually the first one to arrive at school.

* late〔let〕*adj.* 遲到的　　*be late for school* 上學遲到
call〔kɔl〕*v.* 打電話給～　　well〔wɛl〕*interj.* 喔；嗯
fault〔fɔlt〕*n.* 過錯　　*traffic jam* 塞車
besides〔bɪˋsaɪdz〕*adv.* 此外　　*get to* 抵達
on time 準時　　serious〔ˋsɪrɪəs〕*adj.* 嚴重的
usually〔ˋjuʒʊəlɪ〕*adv.* 通常　　arrive〔əˋraɪv〕*v.* 抵達

23. (**C**) M：What are you planning to do for Joan's birthday?

W：I thought we would go out to dinner and then go bowling.

M：That's a good idea. Joan loves bowling.

Question：Why are they going out to dinner?

A. It is a good place to eat dinner.

B. They need energy for bowling.

C. It is Joan's birthday.

* plan〔plæn〕*v.* 計劃　　*go out to dinner* 出去吃晚餐
bowl〔bol〕*v.* 打保齡球　　*good idea* 好主意
energy〔ˋɛnɚdʒɪ〕*n.* 精力；活力

24. (**B**) M: Where is your bag?

W: It's under the seat.

M: Good. Now fasten your seatbelt before we take off.

Question: Where did this conversation take place?

A. In a car.

B. On an airplane.

C. On a boat.

* bag〔bæg〕*n.* 手提袋　under〔'ʌndɚ〕*prep.* 在…之下
  seat〔sit〕*n.* 座位　fasten〔'fæsn̩〕*v.* 繫上
  seatbelt〔'sit,bɛlt〕*n.* 安全帶　***take off*** 起飛
  conversation〔,kɑnvɚ'seʃən〕*n.* 對話
  take place 發生　airplane〔'ɛr,plen〕*n.* 飛機
  boat〔bot〕*n.* 船

25. (**A**) M: What's your cat's name?

W: It's Brad Pitt.

M: Like the movie star?

W: That's right.

Question: What do we know about the woman?

A. She is a fan of Brad Pitt.

B. She is taking care of Brad Pitt's cat.

C. Her cat looks like Brad Pitt's cat.

* ***Brad Pitt*** 布萊德彼特（男星名）
  like〔laɪk〕*prep.* 像…　***movie star*** 電影明星
  fan〔fæn〕*n.* 迷　***take care of*** 照顧
  look like 看起來像

26. (**B**)　M：Will you take these letters to the post office for me?

W：Sure.　I'm going there tomorrow.

M：Uh, it's kind of important.

W：Oh, all right.　I'll do it now.

Question：What will the woman do?

A. She will write an important letter.

B. She will go to the post office right away.

C. She will ask the man to do it right now.

* letter〔ˈlɛtɚ〕 *n.* 信　　***post office*** 郵局
sure〔ʃur〕 *adv.* 好；當然　　uh〔ʌ〕 *interj.* 唔；嗯
kind of 有點　　important〔ɪmˈpɔrtn̩t〕 *adj.* 重要的
oh〔o〕 *interj.* 喔　　***all right*** 好的
right away 馬上　　ask〔æsk〕 *v.* 要求
right now 現在；立刻

27. (**C**)　M：I don't know what to order.

W：Why don't you have a hamburger?

M：No.　I had one for lunch.

Question：Why doesn't the man want to eat a hamburger?

A. Hamburgers should be eaten only at lunchtime.

B. He does not like hamburgers.

C. He doesn't want to eat two hamburgers in one day.

* order〔ˈɔrdɚ〕 *v.* 點菜　　have〔hæv〕 *v.* 吃
hamburger〔ˈhæmbɝɡɚ〕 *n.* 漢堡
lunchtime〔ˈlʌntʃ͵taɪm〕 *n.* 午餐時間

28. (**C**) M：How do you feel?

W：I have a headache and a sore throat.

M：You had better rest. If you don't feel better
tomorrow, go to see a doctor.

Question：What does the man suggest?

A. The woman should see a doctor right away.

B. The woman will feel better tomorrow.

C. The woman should rest.

* feel〔fil〕*v.* 覺得
headache〔'hɛd,ek〕*n.* 頭痛
sore〔sor〕*adj.* 疼痛的
throat〔θrot〕*n.* 喉嚨
had better V. 最好～　　rest〔rɛst〕*v.* 休息
suggest〔səg'dʒɛst〕*v.* 建議

29. (**B**) M：Can you help me find this in a size M?

W：I'm sorry, sir. We sold the last size M this
morning.

M：Oh. Do you have any other jackets in a similar
style?

W：Yes. But they are a lot more expensive.

M：Thank you. I'll try somewhere else.

Question：What will the man do?

A. He will try on a different jacket.

B. He will try to find a jacket in a different store.

C. He will try to get a discount.

* size〔saɪz〕*n.* 尺寸 　　*size M* 中號
M 中號的（衣服）（= *medium* ）
jacket〔'dʒækɪt〕*n.* 夾克
similar〔'sɪmələ〕*adj.* 類似的 　　style〔staɪl〕*n.* 樣式
expensive〔ɪk'spɛnsɪv〕*adj.* 昂貴的
somewhere else 別的地方
try on 試穿 　　different〔'dɪfərənt〕*adj.* 不同的
store〔stor〕*n.* 商店 　　discount〔'dɪskaʊnt〕*n.* 折扣

30. (**C**) M：Where did you park your car?

W：In front of the building.

M：Oh. You had better move it before the police
come along.

Question：Why should the woman move her car?

A. It is a police car.

B. The police told her to move it.

C. Parking is not allowed in front of the building.

* park〔pɑrk〕*v.* 停（車） 　　*in front of* ~ 在~的前面
building〔'bɪldɪŋ〕*n.* 建築物；大樓
move〔muv〕*v.* 移動 　　police〔pə'lis〕*n.* 警察
come along 過來 　　*police car* 警車
allow〔ə'laʊ〕*v.* 允許

全民英語能力分級檢定測驗
初級測驗⑤

　　本測驗分三部份，全爲三選一之選擇題，每部份各 10 題，共 30 題，作答時間約 20 分鐘。

第一部份：看圖辨義

　　　　本部份共 10 題，試題冊上每題有一個圖片，請聽錄音機播出一個相關的問題，與 A、B、C 三個英語敘述後，選一個與所看到圖片最相符的答案，並在答案紙上相對的圓圈內塗黑作答。每題播出一遍，問題及選項均不印在試題冊上。

例：(看)

NT$80　　NT$50

(聽)

Look at the picture.　How much is the hamburger?

　　A.　It's eighty dollars.
　　B.　It's fifty-five dollars.
　　C.　It's eighteen dollars.

正確答案爲 A

<u>Questions 1</u>

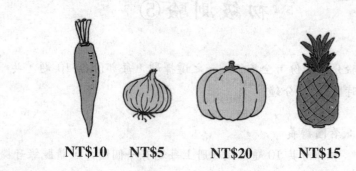

NT$10   NT$5   NT$20   NT$15

<u>Question 2</u>

<u>Question 3</u>

Questions 4

Question 5

請 翻 頁 ◀▭⟹

Question 6

Question 7

Question 8

Question 9

Question 10

請翻頁 ▯▯⟹

第二部份： 問答

　　　本部份共 10 題，每題錄音機會播出一個問句或直述句，
每題播出一次，聽後請從試題冊上 A、B、C 三個選項
中，選出一個最適合的回答或回應，並在答案紙上塗黑
作答。

例：

（聽） Good morning, Kevin.　How are you?

（看）　A.　I'm fine, thank you.
　　　　B.　I'm in the living room.
　　　　C.　My name is Kevin.

　　　正確答案為 A

11. A. About two hours.
　　 B. Not very hard.
　　 C. It's in chemistry.

12. A. No, I've never.
　　 B. Yes.　She wrote
　　　　me last week.
　　 C. Yes, I've heard of
　　　　her.

13. A. No.　I think you are in
　　　　the wrong room.
　　 B. You deserve the prize.
　　 C. I got a good score, too.

14. A. It is in France.
　　 B. I'm sorry.　I don't speak
　　　　French.
　　 C. It leaves from platform 8.

15. A. It's six million dollars.
    B. I would buy a house.
    C. No, I've never won anything.

16. A. Yes. It was great!
    B. It took half an hour.
    C. Yes. I was very good this time.

17. A. The meeting is at two.
    B. Sure. Where?
    C. No. It's not six o'clock yet.

18. A. Of course. She is my classmate.
    B. No. She is my sister.
    C. Yes, I know.

19. A. No thanks. I don't need a new pen.
    B. No, you're not bothering me.
    C. Here you are.

20. A. I don't have a motorbike.
    B. Every day.
    C. Number 11.

請 翻 頁 ▯▭▷

第三部份： 簡短對話

本部份共 10 題，每題錄音機會播出一段對話及一個相關的問題，每題播出兩次，聽後請從試題冊上 A、B、C 三個選項中，選出一個最適合的回答，並在答案紙上塗黑作答。

例：

(聽) (Woman) Good afternoon, …Mr. Davis?

(Man) Yes. I have an appointment with Dr. Sanders at two o'clock. My son Tommy has a fever.

(Woman) Oh, that's too bad. Well, please have a seat, Mr. Davis. Dr. Sanders will be right with you.

Question: Where did this conversation take place?

(看) A. In a post office.

B. In a restaurant.

C. In a doctor's office.

正確答案爲 C

21. A. She usually drives, but
       she sometimes takes
       train.
    B. She often takes a plane
       because flying is cheap.
    C. She often drives and
       never takes a train.

22. A. She can buy it for 100
       dollars.
    B. She borrowed it; she
       did not buy it.
    C. She is going to loan it
       to the store.

23. A. The woman often goes
       skiing there.
    B. Many people go there
       in January.
    C. It usually snows there
       in January.

24. A. She got a prize
       after studying very
       hard.
    B. She won a prize
       she didn't deserve.
    C. She didn't have
       enough time to
       study.

25. A. He doesn't like hot
       weather.
    B. He thinks summer
       is too hot.
    C. He likes to swim
       very much.

26. A. At a summer camp.
    B. At a hotel.
    C. In a hospital.

請 翻 頁 ▌⟹

27. A. She occasionally goes back to her hometown.
    B. She lives far away from her parents.
    C. She misses her family very much.

28. A. She had to spend fifty dollars to buy a notebook.
    B. The clerk did not give her enough money.
    C. The store clerk was very rude to her.

29. A. The woman made it at home.
    B. The woman got it at a supermarket.
    C. The man brought it from his home.

30. A. The store is having a big sale.
    B. She was waiting for the man.
    C. She didn't know what time the store would open.

初級英語聽力檢定⑤詳解

第一部份

Look at the picture for question 1.

1. (**A**) Jan wants to buy a carrot and a pumpkin. How much money will she spend?
   A. Thirty dollars.
   B. Twenty dollars.
   C. Twenty-five dollars.

   * carrot〔'kærət〕 *n.* 紅蘿蔔
     pumpkin〔'pʌmpkɪn〕 *n.* 南瓜
     spend〔spɛnd〕 *v.* 花（錢）　　dollar〔'dɑlɚ〕 *n.* 元

Look at the picture for question 2.

2. (**C**) Why is the girl running?
   A. To the telephone.
   B. She must make a phone call.
   C. The phone is ringing.

   * run〔rʌn〕 *v.* 跑
     telephone〔'tɛlə,fon〕 *n.* 電話（= *phone*）
     must〔mʌst〕 *aux.* 必須
     make a phone call 打一通電話
     ring〔rɪŋ〕 *v.* （鈴）響

Look at the picture for question 3.

3.（**B**）How does the girl feel?

　　A. It is her birthday.

　　B. She is surprised.

　　C. It is for her.

　　＊ feel〔fil〕v. 覺得

　　　surprised〔sə'praɪzd〕adj. 驚訝的

Look at the picture for question 4.

4.（**C**）What is the woman saying?

　　A. She is shaking.

　　B. I am lost.

　　C. Where is the toilet?

　　＊ shake〔ʃek〕v. 發抖　　lost〔lɔst〕adj. 迷路的

　　　toilet〔'tɔɪlɪt〕n. 廁所

Look at the picture for question 5.

5.（**A**）Who wants to go to the mountain?

　　A. The young man.

　　B. By bus.

　　C. To go hiking.

　　＊ mountain〔'maʊntn̩〕n. 山

　　　young〔jʌŋ〕adj. 年輕的

　　　go hiking 去健行；去徒步旅行

Look at the picture for question 6.

6. (**C**) What is the girl looking at?

    A. The dress is beautiful.

    B. She is dancing.

    C. A mirror.

    * *look at* 注視；看著   dress〔drɛs〕*n.* 洋裝
       dance〔dæns〕*v.* 跳舞   mirror〔'mɪrɚ〕*n.* 鏡子

Look at the picture for question 7.

7. (**A**) What time is it?

    A. It is time to go home.

    B. It is almost six o'clock.

    C. It is a new clock.

    * *What time is it?* 現在幾點？
      It is time to~. 是（該~）的時候了。
      almost〔'ɔl,most〕*adv.* 幾乎
      o'clock〔ə'klɑk〕*adv.* …點鐘   clock〔klɑk〕*n.* 時鐘

Look at the picture for question 8.

8. (**B**) Who is pulling it?

    A. Because it is heavy.

    B. A strong man.

    C. A big bag.

    * pull〔pul〕*v.* 拉   heavy〔'hɛvɪ〕*adj.* 重的
      strong〔strɔŋ〕*adj.* 強壯的   bag〔bæg〕*n.* 袋子

Look at the picture for question 9.

9. (**B**) When will it be eight o'clock?

      A. It is eight o'clock now.

      B. In fifteen minutes.

      C. Yes, it is almost eight o'clock.

      * *in fifteen minutes* 再過十五分鐘

Look at the picture for question 10.

10. (**C**) Who is looking out the window?

      A. No, he is looking at a newspaper.

      B. Three people.

      C. A man in the second row.

      * *look out* ~ 往~的外面看　*look at* 看著

      newspaper〔'njuz,pepɚ〕*n.* 報紙

      second〔'sɛkənd〕*adj.* 第二的　　row〔ro〕*n.* 排；列

第二部份

11. (**A**) How long did you study for the test?

      A. About two hours.

      B. Not very hard.

      C. It's in chemistry.

      * *How long* ~ ? ~多久？　about〔ə'baʊt〕*adv.* 大約

      hard〔hɑrd〕*adj.* 困難的

      chemistry〔'kɛmɪstrɪ〕*n.* 化學

12. (**B**) Have you heard from Judy?

    A. No, I've never.

    B. Yes. She wrote me last week.

    C. Yes, I've heard of her.

    * ***hear form*** ~ 得到~的消息；收到~的信

      write [raɪt] *v.* 寫信給人

      hear of 聽說過

13. (**A**) Is this English 101?

    A. No. I think you are in the wrong room.

    B. You deserve the prize.

    C. I got a good score, too.

    * wrong [rɔŋ] *adj.* 錯誤的

      deserve [dɪ'zɜv] *v.* 應得

      prize [praɪz] *n.* 獎   score [skor] *n.* 分數

14. (**C**) Where can I find the train to Paris?

    A. It is in France.

    B. I'm sorry. I don't speak French.

    C. It leaves from platform 8.

    * find [faɪn] *v.* 找到   train [tren] *n.* 火車

      Paris ['pærɪs] *n.* 巴黎   France [fræns] *n.* 法國

      French [frɛntʃ] *n.* 法語

      leave [liv] *v.* 出發；離開

      platform ['plæt,fɔrm] *n.* 月台

15. (**B**)　What would you do if you won the lottery?

　　　　A. It's six million dollars.

　　　　B. I would buy a house.

　　　　C. No, I've never won anything.

　　　* win〔wɪn〕v. 贏得　　lottery〔'lɑtərɪ〕n. 彩券

　　　　million〔'mɪljən〕n. 百萬

　　　　dollar〔'dɑlə〕n. 元

16. (**A**)　Did you have a good time?

　　　　A. Yes. It was great!

　　　　B. It took half an hour.

　　　　C. Yes. I was very good this time.

　　　* *have a good time* 玩得愉快

　　　　take〔tek〕v. 花費（時間）

　　　　half an hour 半小時

　　　　this time 這一次

17. (**B**)　Can you meet me at six o'clock?

　　　　A. The meeting is at two.

　　　　B. Sure. Where?

　　　　C. No. It's not six o'clock yet.

　　　* meet〔mit〕v. 和…見面

　　　　meeting〔'mitɪŋ〕n. 會議

　　　　sure〔ʃur〕adv. 當然；好啊　　*not…yet* 尚未…

18. (**A**) Do you know Paula?

    A. Of course. She is my classmate.

    B. No. She is my sister.

    C. Yes, I know.

    * know〔no〕*v.* 知道;認識　*of course* 當然

    classmate〔'klæs,met〕*n.* 同班同學

19. (**C**) May I borrow your pen?

    A. No thanks. I don't need a new pen.

    B. No, you're not bothering me.

    C. Here you are.

    * may〔me〕*aux.* 可以

    borrow〔'baro〕*v.* 借(入)

    need〔nid〕*v.* 需要　bother〔'baðɚ〕*v.* 打擾

    Here you are. 你要的東西在這裡;拿去吧。

    (= *Here it is.*)

20. (**C**) Which bus do you take to school?

    A. I don't have a motorbike.

    B. Every day.

    C. Number 11.

    * which〔hwɪtʃ〕*pron.* 哪一個　take〔tek〕*v.* 搭乘

    motorbike〔'motɚ,baɪk〕*n.* 機車

    number 11 11 號

第三部份

21. (**C**) M: Have you ever taken a train in the United States?

W: Never. I usually drive, but sometimes I fly.

M: Isn't that expensive?

W: Taking the train is expensive, too.

Question: What is true about the woman when she is in the United States?

A. She usually drives, but she sometimes takes a train.

B. She often takes a plane because flying is cheap.

C. She often drives and never takes a train.

* *the United States* 美國

never〔'nɛvɚ〕*adv.* 從未；不曾

usually〔'juʒʊəlɪ〕*adv.* 通常

drive〔draɪv〕*v.* 開車

sometimes〔'sʌm,taɪmz〕*adv.* 有時候

fly〔flaɪ〕*v.* 搭飛機

expensive〔ɪk'spɛnsɪv〕*adj.* 昂貴的

true〔tru〕*adj.* 真的   often〔'ɔfən〕*adv.* 經常

plane〔plen〕*n.* 飛機

cheap〔tʃip〕*adj.* 便宜的

22. (**B**) M：Did you buy this DVD?

W：No. I rented it from the store downstairs.

M：When do you have to take it back?

W：Tomorrow. Otherwise, I will have to pay a 100 dollar fine.

Question：Why will the woman take the DVD to the store tomorrow?

A. She can buy it for 100 dollars.

B. She borrowed it; she did not buy it.

C. She is going to loan it to the store.

* DVD 數位影音光碟 (= *Digital Video Disc*)
  rent〔rɛnt〕*v.* 租   store〔stor〕*n.* 商店
  downstairs〔'daʊn'stɛrz〕*adv.* 在樓下
  have to 必須   back〔bæk〕*adv.* 返還
  otherwise〔'ʌðə‚waɪz〕*adv.* 否則
  pay〔pe〕*v.* 支付   fine〔faɪn〕*n.* 罰金
  borrow〔'bɑro〕*v.* 借 (入)
  loan〔lon〕*v.* 借 (出)

23. (**C**) M：When are you going to take your vacation?

W：I'm planning to go to Japan in January.

M：But it's so cold then!

W：That's all right. I want to go skiing.

Question：What do we know about Japan?

A. The woman often goes skiing there.

B. Many people go there in January.

C. It usually snows there in January.

* **_take a vacation_** 度假　　plan〔plæn〕_v._ 計劃
　Japan〔dʒə'pæn〕_n._ 日本
　January〔'dʒænju,ɛrɪ〕_n._ 一月
　so〔so〕_adv._ 如此地　　then〔ðɛn〕_adv._ 那時
　That's all right. 沒關係。
　go skiing 去滑雪　　snow〔sno〕_v._ 下雪

24. (**A**)　M：Did you know that Lisa won the first prize in
　　　　　　math?

　　　　W：No, I didn't.　Good for her.

　　　　M：She deserves it.　She studies all the time.

　　　Question：What happened to Lisa?

　　A. She got a prize after studying very hard.

　　B. She won a prize she didn't deserve.

　　C. She didn't have enough time to study.

* win〔wɪn〕_v._ 贏得　　**_first prize_** 頭獎；第一名
　math〔mæθ〕_n._ 數學（= _mathematics_）
　Good for her. 她真行；幹得好！
　deserve〔dɪ'zɜv〕_v._ 應得
　all the time 經常；始終　　happen〔'hæpən〕_v._ 發生

25. (**C**) M：Which is your favorite season?

　　　　W：I like spring the best because the weather is not too hot.

　　　　M：Oh, not me! I like summer because it's hot enough to swim.

　　　Question：What is true about the man?

　　　A. He doesn't like hot weather.

　　　B. He thinks summer is too hot.

　　　C. He likes to swim very much.

　　　* favorite (ˈfevərɪt) adj. 最喜愛的　　season (ˈsizn̩) n. 季節
　　　　spring (sprɪŋ) n. 春天　　*like ~ the best* 最喜歡~
　　　　weather (ˈwɛðɚ) n. 天氣　　summer (ˈsʌmɚ) n. 夏天
　　　　swim (swɪm) v. 游泳　　true (tru) adj. 正確的

26. (**B**) M：Do you have any rooms available this weekend?

　　　　W：Summer is our busiest time, but we do have some rooms free on Saturday.

　　　　M：Great. Please give us the best room available.

　　　Question：Where does the woman work?

　　　A. At a summer camp.

　　　B. At a hotel.

　　　C. In a hospital.

　　　* available (əˈveləbl̩) adj. 可獲得的；可使用的
　　　　weekend (ˈwikˌɛnd) n. 週末　　free (fri) adj. 空著的
　　　　great (gret) adj. 太好了　　*summer camp* 夏令營
　　　　hotel (hoˈtɛl) n. 旅館　　hospital (ˈhɑspɪtl̩) n. 醫院

27. (**A**)　M：Do you have a lot of family in town?

W：No.　My parents moved here from the south about five years ago.　Most of my relatives still live down there.

M：How often do you see them?

W：We go back on most big holidays.

Question：What do we know about the woman?

A.　She occasionally goes back to her hometown.

B.　She lives far away from her parents.

C.　She misses her family very much.

* family〔'fæməlɪ〕 *n.* 家人

town〔taʊn〕 *n.* 城鎮

parents〔'pɛrənts〕 *n. pl.* 父母

move〔muv〕 *v.* 搬家　　south〔saʊθ〕 *n.* 南方

most of ~　大部份的~

relative〔'rɛlətɪv〕 *n.* 親戚

down〔daʊn〕 *adv.* 在南方

How often ~ *?*　~多久一次？

go back　回去　　holiday〔'hɑlə‚de〕 *n.* 節日

occasionally〔ə'keʒənḷɪ〕 *adv.* 偶爾

hometown〔'hom'taʊn〕 *n.* 家鄉

far away from ~　離~很遠

miss〔mɪs〕 *v.* 想念

28. (**B**) M：You look upset. What's the matter?

W：I think the clerk gave me the wrong change.

M：How much did you give him?

W：I gave him one thousand for a fifty-dollar notebook, but he only gave me four hundred and fifty dollars back.

Question：Why is the woman unhappy?

A. She had to spend fifty dollars to buy a notebook.

B. The clerk did not give her enough money.

C. The store clerk was very rude to her.

* look〔lʊk〕v. 看起來　　upset〔ʌpˈsɛt〕adj. 不高興的

What's the matter? 怎麼了？

clerk〔klɝk〕n. 店員　　wrong〔rɔŋ〕adj. 錯誤的

change〔tʃendʒ〕n. 找的錢

thousand〔ˈθaʊznd〕n. 千

notebook〔ˈnotˌbʊk〕n. 筆記本

hundred〔ˈhʌndrəd〕n. 百

unhappy〔ʌnˈhæpɪ〕adj. 不高興的

enough〔əˈnʌf〕adj. 足夠的

rude〔rud〕adj. 無禮的；粗魯的

29. (**B**) M：This is a great apple pie. How did you make it?

W：I didn't. I bought it at the supermarket.

M：Really? But it tastes homemade.

Question：Where did the pie come from?

A. The woman made it at home.

B. The woman got it at a supermarket.

C. The man brought it from his home.

* great〔gret〕*adj.* 很棒的　　***apple pie*** 蘋果派
　 supermarket〔'supɚ͵mɑrkɪt〕*n.* 超級市場
　 Really? 真的嗎？（尾音上揚）
　 taste〔test〕*v.* 嚐起來
　 homemade〔'hom'med〕*adj.* 自家做的
　 get〔gɛt〕*v.* 買

30. (**A**)　M：Have they opened the doors yet?

　　　　　W：No.　The store doesn't open until 10:00.

　　　　　M：How long have you been waiting here?

　　　　　W：About an hour.

　　　　　M：Wow!　This must be some great sale!

　　　　Question：Why did the woman wait outside the store
　　　　　　　　　for an hour?

A. The store is having a big sale.

B. She was waiting for the man.

C. She didn't know what time the store would open.

* yet〔jɛt〕*adv.* 已經（用於疑問句）
　 not…until~ 直到～才…　　***How long~?*** ～多久？
　 wait〔wet〕*v.* 等待　　wow〔waʊ〕*interj.* 哇
　 must〔mʌst〕*aux.* 一定　　some〔sʌm〕*adv.* 某個
　 great〔gret〕*adj.* 很大的　　sale〔sel〕*n.* 拍賣
　 outside〔'aʊt'saɪd〕*prep.* 在～的外面

全民英語能力分級檢定測驗
初級測驗⑥

　　本測驗分三部份，全為三選一之選擇題，每部份各 10 題，共 30 題，作答時間約 20 分鐘。

第一部份：看圖辨義
　　　　　本部份共 10 題，試題冊上每題有一個圖片，請聽錄音機播出一個相關的問題，與 A、B、C 三個英語敘述後，選一個與所看到圖片最相符的答案，並在答案紙上相對的圓圈內塗黑作答。每題播出一遍，問題及選項均不印在試題冊上。

例：（看）

NT$80　NT$50

（聽）

Look at the picture.　How much is the hamburger?

　　A.　It's eighty dollars.
　　B.　It's fifty-five dollars.
　　C.　It's eighteen dollars.

正確答案為 A

Questions 1

Question 2

Question 3

Questions 4

Question 5

請翻頁 ▯▭⇒

Question 6

Question 7

Question 8

Question 9

Question 10

請 翻 頁 ▯▭▷

第二部份： 問答

本部份共 10 題，每題錄音機會播出一個問句或直述句，
每題播出一次，聽後請從試題冊上 A、B、C 三個選項
中，選出一個最適合的回答或回應，並在答案紙上塗黑
作答。

例：

（聽） Good morning, Kevin. How are you?

（看） A. I'm fine, thank you.
B. I'm in the living room.
C. My name is Kevin.

正確答案為 A

11. A. It's four o'clock.
B. It's on the table.
C. I can't. It's too small.

12. A. Yes, please.
B. Water, please.
C. Waiter!

13. A. No, I don't have a key.
B. Yes, it is.
C. Yes, I locked it.

14. A. It takes 10 minutes to get there.
B. Every 15 minutes.
C. In five minutes.

15. A. Yes, I am.

    B. Who knows?

    C. Nice to meet you.

16. A. Here's twenty.

    B. I only have

       seventy-five.

    C. I will, too.

17. A. But it's not that cold.

    B. It's not my size.

    C. Right away.

18. A. Yes, I was.

    B. No, I couldn't.

    C. Sure I would.

19. A. I'm thirteen.

    B. In April.

    C. At three o'clock.

20. A. Our new classmate.

    B. Pleased to meet you.

    C. He is much better

       now.

請 翻 頁 ⅠⅡ⇒

第三部份： 簡短對話

本部份共 10 題，每題錄音機會播出一段對話及一個相關的問題，每題播出兩次，聽後請從試題冊上 A、B、C 三個選項中，選出一個最適合的回答，並在答案紙上塗黑作答。

例：

（聽）(Woman) Good afternoon, …Mr. Davis?

　　　(Man) Yes. I have an appointment with Dr. Sanders at two o'clock. My son Tommy has a fever.

　　　(Woman) Oh, that's too bad. Well, please have a seat, Mr. Davis. Dr. Sanders will be right with you.

　　　Question: Where did this conversation take place?

（看）A. In a post office.

　　　B. In a restaurant.

　　　C. In a doctor's office.

正確答案為 C

21. A. Eat the cake alone.
    B. Eat all of the cake.
    C. Go on a diet.

22. A. The man won the game.
    B. By one point.
    C. The woman's team.

23. A. Three days from now.
    B. Today.
    C. As soon as she fills out the form.

24. A. The salad is very good.
    B. He is overweight.
    C. He doesn't like pizza.

25. A. It is too late to take a taxi.
    B. She thinks taxis are not expensive.
    C. She does not want to spend money on a taxi.

26. A. They will give Mimi a puppy if she is good.
    B. The woman has a new dog.
    C. The woman behaves very well.

請 翻 頁 ⟹

27. A. She prefers tennis to soccer.
　　B. She is not good at soccer.
　　C. She does not have enough time for soccer.

28. A. He wants to eat lunch.
　　B. He wants to know where the cafeteria is.
　　C. He wants to find Mrs. West.

29. A. He lives near the woman now.
　　B. He is the woman's cousin.
　　C. He would like to meet George.

30. A. He wants to buy a flower.
　　B. He wants to find a bakery.
　　C. He wants to bake something.

初級英語聽力檢定⑥詳解

第一部份

Look at the picture for question 1.

1. (**C**) Where is the boy reading?
    A. It is a textbook.
    B. He is too sleepy.
    C. In a library.

    * textbook〔'tɛkst,bʊk〕n. 教科書
      sleepy〔'slipɪ〕adj. 想睡的；睏的
      library〔'laɪ,brɛrɪ〕n. 圖書館

Look at the picture for question 2.

2. (**C**) How is the weather?
    A. It is winter.　　　B. He is five.
    C. It is cold.

    * weather〔'wɛðɚ〕n. 天氣　　winter〔'wɪntɚ〕n. 冬天
      five〔faɪv〕adj. 五歲的　　cold〔kold〕adj. 寒冷的

Look at the picture for question 3.

3. (**A**) How does the woman feel?
    A. Cold.　　　　B. Windy.
    C. Shaking.

    * windy〔'wɪndɪ〕adj. 風大的　　shake〔ʃek〕v. 發抖

Look at the picture for question 4.

4. (**C**) Why does the man need help?

  A. The bag is too heavy.

  B. Yes, he does.

  C. He cannot find the museum.

  * bag〔bæg〕*n.* 袋子 heavy〔'hɛvɪ〕*adj.* 重的
  find〔faɪd〕*v.* 找到
  museum〔mju'ziəm〕*n.* 博物館

Look at the picture for question 5.

5. (**B**) Who is it chasing?

  A. A dog.

  B. A man.

  C. A house.

  * chase〔tʃes〕*v.* 追逐

Look at the picture for question 6.

6. (**B**) What happened to the boy?

  A. He is crying.

  B. He dropped his ice cream.

  C. He ate too much ice cream.

  * ***happen to*** 發生在…身上 cry〔kraɪ〕*v.* 哭
  drop〔drɑp〕*v.* 使…落下 ***ice cream*** 冰淇淋

Look at the picture for question 7.

7. (**C**) Who is wet?

    A. The ground.

    B. Because it was raining.

    C. A man.

    * wet〔wɛt〕*adj.* 濕的   ground〔graʊnd〕*n.* 地面

    because〔bɪ'kɔz〕*conj.* 因為

    rain〔ren〕*v.* 下雨

Look at the picture for question 8.

8. (**A**) What time of day is it?

    A. It is the middle of the night.

    B. It is afternoon.

    C. It is on the wall.

    * time〔taɪm〕*n.* 時候   middle〔'mɪdl̩〕*n.* 中間

    the middle of the night 半夜

    wall〔wɔl〕*n.* 牆壁

Look at the picture for question 9.

9. (**B**) Where is the pot?

    A. It is steam.

    B. On the stove.

    C. It is cooking.

    * pot〔pɑt〕*n.* 鍋;壺   steam〔stim〕*n.* 蒸氣

    stove〔stov〕*n.* 爐子   cook〔kʊk〕*v.* 烹煮

Look at the picture for question 10.

10. (**C**) Who is introducing the girl?

    A. Yes, they are.

    B. Yes, she is.

    C. The boy in the middle.

    * introduce〔͵ɪntrə'djus〕v. 介紹

第二部份

11. (**B**) Have you seen my watch?

    A. It's four o'clock.

    B. It's on the table.

    C. I can't. It's too small.

    * watch〔watʃ〕n. 手錶

12. (**B**) What do you want to drink?

    A. Yes, please.

    B. Water, please.

    C. Waiter!

    * drink〔drɪŋk〕v. 喝　waiter〔'wetɚ〕n. 服務生

13. (**A**) Can you unlock the door?

    A. No, I don't have a key.

    B. Yes, it is.

    C. Yes, I locked it.

    * unlock〔ʌn'lɑk〕v. 打開…的鎖　lock〔lɑk〕v. 鎖

14. (**B**) How often does the bus come?

    A. It takes 10 minutes to get there.

    B. Every 15 minutes.

    C. In five minutes.

    * *How often~?* ～多久一次？

      take〔tek〕v. 花費（時間）　　get〔gɛt〕v. 抵達

      Every 15 minutes. 每隔十五分鐘。

      In five minutes. 再過五分鐘。

15. (**C**) This is my sister Judy.

    A. Yes, I am.

    B. Who knows?

    C. Nice to meet you.

    * *Nice to meet you.* 很高興認識妳。

16. (**A**) That will be eighteen dollars.

    A. Here's twenty.

    B. I only have seventy-five.

    C. I will, too.

    * dollar〔'dɑlɚ〕n. 元　　only〔'onlɪ〕adv. 只有

17. (**C**) Please hang up your jacket.

    A. But it's not that cold.

    B. It's not my size.

    C. Right away.

    * *hang up* 掛起　　jacket〔'dʒækɪt〕n. 夾克

      size〔saɪz〕n. 尺寸　　*Right away.* 馬上；立刻

18. (**B**) Did you watch *Survivor* last night?

    A. Yes, I was.

    B. No, I couldn't.

    C. Sure I would.

    * watch〔watʃ〕v. 看（電視）

    Survivor〔sə'vaɪvɚ〕n. 倖存者（美國電視節目，台灣譯爲

    《我要活下去》）

19. (**B**) When is your birthday?

    A. I'm thirteen.

    B. In April.

    C. At three o'clock.

    * April〔'eprəl〕n. 四月

20. (**A**) Who is that boy?

    A. Our new classmate.

    B. Pleased to meet you.

    C. He is much better now.

    * classmate〔'klæs,met〕n. 同班同學

    pleased〔plizd〕adj. 高興的

    Pleased to meet you. 很高興認識你。

    much better 好很多

第三部份

21. (**C**)　M：What did the doctor say?

　　　　W：He said I should lose some weight.

　　　　M：Too bad.　I'll have to eat this cake all by myself.

　　　Question：What does the woman have to do?

　　　A. Eat the cake alone.

　　　B. Eat all of the cake.

　　　C. Go on a diet.

　　　* lose〔luz〕*v.* 減少　　weight〔wet〕*n.* 體重
　　　lose weight 減肥　　*too bad* 真糟糕
　　　have to 必須　　*all by* oneself 獨自；靠自己
　　　alone〔ə'lon〕*adv.* 獨自地　　*go on a diet* 進行節食

22. (**C**)　M：How was the game?

　　　　W：It was very exciting.　The score was 98 to 97.

　　　　M：But who won?

　　　　W：Oh, my team won, of course!

　　　Question：Who won the game?

　　　A. The man won the game.

　　　B. By one point.

　　　C. The woman's team.

　　　* game〔gem〕*n.* 比賽　　exciting〔ɪk'saɪtɪŋ〕*adj.* 刺激的
　　　score〔skor〕*n.* 分數　　to〔tu〕*prep.* …比… (表對比)
　　　win〔wɪn〕*v.* 贏 (三態變化為：win-won-won)
　　　team〔tim〕*n.* 隊　　*of course* 當然
　　　by one point 差一分

23. (**A**) M：Do you have a library card?

W：No, I don't.

M：Then fill out this form, please.

W：Okay. When will I get the card?

M：In about three days, but I'll let you borrow a book today if you like.

Question：When will the woman get her library card?

A. Three days from now.

B. Today.

C. As soon as she fills out the form.

* library〔'laɪ,brɛrɪ〕 *n.* 圖書館

card〔kɑrd〕 *n.* 卡；卡片

library card 借書證　　***fill out*** 填寫

form〔fɔrm〕 *n.* 表格

okay〔'o'ke〕 *interj.* 好（= *OK*）

borrow〔'bɑro〕 *v.* 借（入）

if you like 如果你想要；如果你願意

three days from now 三天之後

as soon as 一…就～

24. (**B**) M：What should we eat?

W：How about pizza?

M：No, thanks. I'm trying to lose weight.

W：We could go to the salad bar.

M：That's a good idea.

Question：Why does the man want to eat salad?

A. The salad is very good.

B. He is overweight.

C. He doesn't like pizza.

* *How about ～?* ～如何？

salad〔'sæləd〕*n.* 沙拉　　**salad bar** 沙拉吧

overweight〔'ovɚ'wet〕*adj.* 過重的

25. (**C**) M：Let's take a bus downtown.

W：We can't. They stop running at ten o'clock.

M：Then we'll have to take a taxi.

W：Only if you're paying.

Question：What does the woman mean?

A. It is too late to take a taxi.

B. She thinks taxis are not expensive.

C. She does not want to spend money on a taxi.

* take〔tek〕*v.* 搭乘

downtown〔'daun'taun〕*adv.* 到市中心

stop + V-ing 停止～

run〔rʌn〕*v.*（交通工具定時地）行駛

then〔ðɛn〕*adv.* 那麼　　taxi〔'tæksɪ〕*n.* 計程車

only if～ 除非～　　pay〔pe〕*v.* 付錢

too～to… 太～以致不能…

expensive〔ɪk'spɛnsɪv〕*adj.* 昂貴的

spend〔spɛnd〕*v.* 花（錢）

26. (**B**) M：Who's this?

W：This is Mimi. Isn't she cute?

M：Sure is. And she's very well behaved for a puppy.

Question：Which of the following is true?

A. They will give Mimi a puppy if she is good.

B. The woman has a new dog.

C. The woman behaves very well.

* cute〔kjut〕adj. 可愛的　　sure〔ʃʊr〕adv. 的確

Sure is. 是 It sure is. 的省略。

well behaved 守規矩的

puppy〔'pʌpɪ〕n.（未滿一歲的）小狗

following〔'fɑləwɪŋ〕adj. 以下的

the following 以下的事物

good〔gʊd〕adj. 乖的

behave〔bɪ'hev〕v. 行為舉止

well〔wɛl〕adv. 良好地

27. (**C**) M：Why didn't you join the soccer team?

W：They have to practice five days a week.

M：So what will you do instead?

W：I joined the tennis team.

Question：Why did the woman join the tennis team?

A. She prefers tennis to soccer.

B. She is not good at soccer.

C. She does not have enough time for soccer.

> * join〔dʒɔɪn〕v. 加入　　soccer〔'sɑkə〕n. 足球
> team〔tim〕n. 隊　　practice〔'præktɪs〕v. 練習
> instead〔ɪn'stɛd〕adv. 作為代替　　tennis〔'tɛnɪs〕n. 網球
> **prefer** A **to** B 比較喜歡 A，而比較不喜歡 B；喜歡 A 甚於 B
> **be good at** 擅長　　enough〔ə'nʌf〕adj. 足夠的

28. (**C**)　M：Do you know where Mrs. West is?

　　　　　W：I think she's in the office.

　　　　　M：No, she isn't.

　　　　　W：Then she must have gone to lunch.

　　　　　M：Thanks. I'll look in the cafeteria.

　　　　　Question：What does the man want?

　　　　　A. He wants to eat lunch.

　　　　　B. He wants to know where the cafeteria is.

　　　　　C. He wants to find Mrs. West.

> * Mrs.〔'mɪsɪz〕n. 太太；夫人 (加在已婚女士的姓之前)
> office〔'ɔfɪs〕n. 辦公室　　look〔lʊk〕v. 看 (有尋找之意)
> cafeteria〔ˌkæfə'tɪrɪə〕n. 自助餐廳　　find〔faɪnd〕v. 找到

29. (**A**)　M：Hi. I'm Tim, George's cousin.

　　　　　W：Nice to meet you, Tim. Where are you from?

　　　　　M：Chicago. But we just moved here last week.

　　　　　W：Well, welcome to the neighborhood.

　　　　　M：Thanks.

Question: What do we know about Tim?

A. He lives near the woman now.

B. He is the woman's cousin.

C. He would like to meet George.

* hi〔haɪ〕*interj.* 嗨　　cousin〔'kʌzn̩〕*n.* 表（堂）兄弟姊妹
  Nice to meet you. 很高興認識你。
  Where are you from? 你是哪裡人？
  Chicago〔ʃə'kɑgo〕*n.* 芝加哥（位於美國伊利諾州）
  move〔muv〕*v.* 搬家　　well〔wɛl〕*interj.* 嗯
  welcome to～ 歡迎來到～
  neighborhood〔'nebə,hʊd〕*n.* 鄰近地區；附近
  near〔nɪr〕*prep.* 在…附近
  would like to V. 想要～（= *want to V.*）
  meet〔mit〕*v.* 和～見面；認識（三態變化為：meet-met-met）

30.(**C**) M: Excuse me. I'm looking for some flour.

W: Everything for baking is in aisle two. The flour
is next to the sugar.

M: Thanks a lot.

Question: What does the man want?

A. He wants to buy a flower.

B. He wants to find a bakery.

C. He wants to bake something.

* ***Excuse me.*** 不好意思；請問一下。
  look for 尋找　　flour〔flaʊr〕*n.* 麵粉
  bake〔bek〕*v.* 烘焙　　aisle〔aɪl〕*n.* 通道
  next to～ 在～旁邊　　sugar〔'ʃʊgə〕*n.* 糖
  bakery〔'bekərɪ〕*n.* 麵包店

全民英語能力分級檢定測驗

初級測驗⑦

　　本測驗分三部份，全為三選一之選擇題，每部份各 10 題，共 30 題，作答時間約 20 分鐘。

第一部份：看圖辨義

　　　　本部份共 10 題，試題冊上每題有一個圖片，請聽錄音機播出一個相關的問題，與 A、B、C 三個英語敘述後，選一個與所看到圖片最相符的答案，並在答案紙上相對的圓圈內塗黑作答。每題播出一遍，問題及選項均不印在試題冊上。

例：（看）

NT$80　　NT$50

（聽）

Look at the picture.　How much is the hamburger?

　　A. It's eighty dollars.
　　B. It's fifty-five dollars.
　　C. It's eighteen dollars.

正確答案為 A

Questions 1

Question 2

Questions 3

Question 4

Question 5

Question 6

請 翻 頁 ▯▯⟹

Question 7

Question 8

Question 9

Question 10

第二部份： 問答

本部份共 10 題，每題錄音機會播出一個問句或直述句，

每題播出一次，聽後請從試題冊上 A、B、C 三個選項

中，選出一個最適合的回答或回應，並在答案紙上塗黑

作答。

例：

（聽）Good morning, Kevin. How are you?

（看）A. I'm fine, thank you.

B. I'm in the living room.

C. My name is Kevin.

正確答案為 A

11. A. Oh, you're so careless.

B. Thanks. You saved me a lot of trouble.

C. You're right! I dropped.

12. A. Who's calling?

B. Thanks, but you shouldn't have.

C. I already have one.

13. A. My sister's name is Lucy.

B. No. She's not here today.

C. Yes, I have a sister.

14. A. I did, too.

B. Already.

C. Not yet.

15. A. My mother.
    B. At the post office.
    C. I didn't write it.

16. A. It's a diamond.
    B. Last week.
    C. It was a gift.

17. A. No, thanks. I've
       already read it.
    B. Please hurry up and
       finish.
    C. Yes, I'll finish on
       time.

18. A. In the fall semester.
    B. Either computers or
       business.
    C. No, it's too expensive.

19. A. Yes, next week.
    B. Yes, I was.
    C. Yes, I have.

20. A. It was very easy.
    B. For forty-five minutes.
    C. Once a week.

請 翻 頁

第三部份：　簡短對話

本部份共 10 題，每題錄音機會播出一段對話及一個相關的問題，每題播出兩次，聽後請從試題冊上 A、B、C 三個選項中，選出一個最適合的回答，並在答案紙上塗黑作答。

例：

(聽) (Woman)　Good afternoon, ...Mr. Davis?

(Man)　　Yes.　I have an appointment with Dr. Sanders at two o'clock.　My son Tommy has a fever.

(Woman)　Oh, that's too bad.　Well, please have a seat, Mr. Davis.　Dr. Sanders will be right with you.

Question:　Where did this conversation take place?

(看) A.　In a post office.
　　B.　In a restaurant.
　　C.　In a doctor's office.

正確答案為 C

21. A. In a classroom.
    B. In a car.
    C. On a train.

22. A. He received a long-distance phone call.
    B. He wanted to call his brother in Australia.
    C. He wanted to see his brother.

23. A. Why the test is next week.
    B. If he can take the test the next week instead.
    C. When the test will be given.

24. A. The children's shoe department.
    B. His daughter's shoes.
    C. His daughter.

25. A. He finished it.
    B. It was very interesting.
    C. He thinks he should finish it.

26. A. Black coffee.
    B. A glass of milk.
    C. Coffee with milk and sugar.

請 翻 頁 ⅡⅠ⟹

27. A. He is surprised that
the woman won.
B. The woman deserved
to win.
C. The woman should
have won, but she
didn't.

28. A. She is a mechanic.
B. She is a driver.
C. She is an engineer.

29. A. It is a delivery
company.
B. In a flower shop.
C. She will deliver
them to the address.

30. A. They are outside.
B. They are too noisy.
C. They are talking on
the phone.

初級英語聽力檢定⑦詳解

第一部份

Look at the picture for question 1.

1. (**C**)　What will the boy do?
　　　A. He is growing a plant.
　　　B. He is a gardener.
　　　C. Give the plant some water.

　　　*　grow〔gro〕v. 種植　　plant〔plænt〕n. 植物
　　　　gardener〔'gɑrdn̩ə˞〕n. 園丁

Look at the picture for question 2.

2. (**B**)　What is the second place winner wearing?
　　　A. She is wearing a skirt.
　　　B. She is wearing a swimsuit.
　　　C. She is wearing shorts.

　　　*　*second place* 第二名　　winner〔'wɪnə˞〕n. 優勝者
　　　　wear〔wɛr〕v. 穿　　skirt〔skɝt〕n. 裙子
　　　　swimsuit〔'swɪm,sut〕n. 泳衣　　shorts〔ʃɔrts〕n. pl. 短褲

Look at the picture for question 3.

3. (**C**)　What did the chicken do with the egg?
　　　A. Yes, it did.
　　　B. Because there is only one.
　　　C. It laid it.

　　　*　lay〔le〕v. 生（蛋）（三態變化爲：lay-laid-laid）
　　　　chicken〔'tʃɪkən〕n. 雞

Look at the picture for question 4.

4. (**A**)　What did the boy do?

　　　　　A.　He kicked the ball.

　　　　　B.　They are playing soccer.

　　　　　C.　He will catch it.

　　　　＊ kick〔kɪk〕v. 踢　　　soccer〔'sɑkɚ〕n. 足球
　　　　　play soccer 踢足球　　catch〔kætʃ〕v. 接住

Look at the picture for question 5.

5. (**B**)　What is he doing?

　　　　　A.　They are socks.

　　　　　B.　Putting on clothes.

　　　　　C.　On the floor.

　　　　＊ socks〔sɑks〕n. pl. 襪子　　***put on*** 穿上
　　　　　clothes〔kloðz〕n. pl. 衣服　　floor〔flor〕n. 地板

Look at the picture for question 6.

6. (**C**)　What happened to the boy's thumb?

　　　　　A.　It held the hammer.

　　　　　B.　He bit it.

　　　　　C.　He hurt it with the hammer.

　　　　＊ happen〔'hæpən〕v. 發生　　thumb〔θʌm〕n. 大姆指
　　　　　hold〔hold〕v. 握住；拿著　　hammer〔'hæmɚ〕n. 鐵鎚
　　　　　bite〔baɪt〕v. 咬（三態變化爲：bite-bit-bitten/bit）
　　　　　hurt〔hɝt〕v. 傷害；使受傷

Look at the picture for question 7.

7. (**B**) What does the man think?

    A. His job is finished.

    B. It is too late to do that work.

    C. It is only 5:00.

    * job〔dʒɑb〕*n.* 工作　　finished〔'fɪnɪʃt〕*adj.* 完成的

    too…to~ 太…以致不能~

    only〔'onlɪ〕*adv.* 只不過~而已

Look at the picture for question 8.

8. (**C**) What is the woman doing?

    A. She is at home.

    B. It is a lamp.

    C. She is going out.

    * lamp〔læmp〕*n.* 燈　　***go out*** 出去

Look at the picture for question 9.

9. (**A**) How does his mother feel?

    A. She is upset.

    B. She is proud.

    C. He is working too hard.

    * upset〔ʌp'sɛt〕*adj.* 不高興的

    proud〔praʊd〕*adj.* 驕傲的

    work〔wɝk〕*v.* 工作；用功

    hard〔hɑrd〕*adv.* 努力地

Look at the picture for question 10.

10. (**B**) Who is in the room?

      A. It is a classroom.

      B. Many students.

      C. They are taking a test.

      * classroom〔'klæs,rum〕*n.* 教室　　*take a test* 參加考試

第二部份

11. (**B**) Excuse me! You dropped this.

      A. Oh, you're so careless.

      B. Thanks. You saved me a lot of trouble.

      C. You're right! I dropped.

      * ***Excuse me!*** 不好意思；對不起！

      drop〔drɑp〕*v.* 掉落　　oh〔o〕*interj.* 喔

      careless〔'kɛrlɪs〕*adj.* 粗心的

      save〔sev〕*v.* 使（人）省去（麻煩等）

      trouble〔'trʌbl̩〕*n.* 麻煩　　right〔raɪt〕*adj.* 對的

12. (**A**) There's a telephone call for you.

      A. Who's calling?

      B. Thanks, but you shouldn't have.

      C. I already have one.

      * ***There is a telephone call for you.*** 你的電話；有人打電

      話找你。　　call〔kɔl〕*v.* 打電話

      Who's calling?（電話用語）請問哪位？

      already〔ɔl'rɛdɪ〕*adv.* 已經

13. (**B**) Is that your sister?

    A. My sister's name is Lucy.

    B. No. She's not here today.

    C. Yes, I have a sister.

14. (**C**) Did you finish your homework?

    A. I did, too.

    B. Already.

    C. Not yet.

    * finish〔'fɪnɪʃ〕v. 完成

    homework〔'hom‚wɜk〕n. 家庭作業

    Not yet. 還沒。

15. (**A**) Who is the letter from?

    A. My mother.

    B. At the post office.

    C. I didn't write it.

    * *Who is the letter from?* 誰寄來的信？

    post office 郵局　　write〔raɪt〕v. 寫

16. (**C**) Where did you find that ring?

    A. It's a diamond.

    B. Last week.

    C. It was a gift.

    * find〔faɪnd〕v. 找到　　ring〔rɪŋ〕n. 戒指

    diamond〔'daɪəmənd〕n. 鑽石

    gift〔gɪft〕n. 禮物

17. (**A**) I'm finished with the newspaper if you want it.

  A. No, thanks. I've already read it.

  B. Please hurry up and finish.

  C. Yes, I'll finish on time.

  * *be finished with* ～ 用完～（在此指「看完～」）
  newspaper（'njuz,pepɚ）*n.* 報紙
  already（ɔl'rɛdɪ）*adv.* 已經 *hurry up* 趕快
  finish（'fɪnɪʃ）*v.* 完成；做完（在此指「看完」）
  on time 準時

18. (**B**) What will you study in Canada?

  A. In the fall semester.

  B. Either computers or business.

  C. No, it's too expensive.

  * study（'stʌdɪ）*v.* 研讀 Canada（'kænədə）*n.* 加拿大
  fall（fɔl）*n.* 秋天 semester（sə'mɛstɚ）*n.* 學期
  either…or ～ 不是…就是～
  computer（kəm'pjutɚ）*n.* 電腦
  business（'bɪznɪs）*n.* 商業
  expensive（ɪk'spɛnsɪv）*adj.* 昂貴的

19. (**C**) Have you been to Mount Ali?

  A. Yes, next week.

  B. Yes, I was.

  C. Yes, I have.

  * *have been to* ～ 曾經去過～
  Mount Ali 阿里山（= *Mt. Ali*）

20. (**B**) How long should I bake the pie?

A. It was very easy.

B. For forty-five minutes.

C. Once a week.

* ***How long～?*** ～多久？   bake〔bek〕*v.* 烘焙

pie〔paɪ〕*n.* 派   easy〔'izɪ〕*adj.* 容易的

「for＋時間」表「持續～」。

once a week 一個星期一次

第三部份

21. (**B**) M：Why are you stopping?

W：I think we're lost. Where is the map?

M：Here it is.

Question：Where did this conversation take place?

A. In a classroom.

B. In a car.

C. On a train.

* stop〔stɑp〕*v.* 停下來   think〔θɪŋk〕*v.* 認為

lost〔lɔst〕*adj.* 迷路的   map〔mæp〕*n.* 地圖

Here it is. 在這裡；這就是。

conversation〔ˌkɑnvɚ'seʃən〕*n.* 對話

take place 發生   train〔tren〕*n.* 火車

22. (**A**) M: I'm so sorry I'm late.

W: That's all right, but what happened?

M: My brother called just as I was about to leave.

W: Your brother in Australia?

M: That's right. It's been so long since I've talked to him that I couldn't just hang up.

Question: Why was the man late?

A. He received a long-distance phone call.

B. He wanted to call his brother in Australia.

C. He wanted to see his brother.

* late〔let〕*adj.* 遲到的

That's all right. 沒關係。

happen〔'hæpən〕*v.* 發生

call〔kɔl〕*v.* 打電話給~   ***just as*** 正當

be about to V. 即將要~

leave〔liv〕*v.* 離開

Australia〔ɔ'streljə〕*n.* 澳洲

That's right. 沒錯。   long〔lɔŋ〕*adj.* 久的

since〔sɪns〕*conj.* 自從   ***hang up*** 掛斷電話

receive〔rɪ'siv〕*v.* 接到；收到

a long-distance phone call 一通長途電話

23. (**C**) M：Do you know when the next test is?

W：I think it's next week, but I'm not sure.

M：I'll ask the professor.

Question：What will the man ask the professor?

A. Why the test is next week.

B. If he can take the test the next week instead.

C. When the test will be given.

* test〔tɛst〕*n.* 測驗；考試　　think〔θɪŋk〕*v.* 認為
sure〔ʃʊr〕*adj.* 確定的　　ask〔æsk〕*v.* 問
professor〔prəˈfɛsə〕*n.* 教授
take a test 參加考試　　***give a test*** 舉行考試
instead〔ɪnˈstɛd〕*adv.* 作為代替

24. (**A**) M：Where can I find shoes for my daughter?

W：Children's clothing is on the third floor, sir.

M：Thank you.

Question：What is the man looking for?

A. The children's shoe department.

B. His daughter's shoes.

C. His daughter.

* find〔faɪnd〕*v.* 找到　　shoes〔ʃuz〕*n. pl.* 鞋子
daughter〔ˈdɔtə〕*n.* 女兒
clothing〔ˈkloðɪŋ〕*n.* 衣物
floor〔flor〕*n.* 樓層　　***look for*** 尋找
department〔dɪˈpɑrtmənt〕*n.* 部門

25. (**B**) M：Did you finish that book?

W：No. It wasn't very interesting.

M：Really? I thought it was great.

Question：What does the man think of the book?

A. He finished it.

B. It was very interesting.

C. He thinks he should finish it.

* finish〔ˈfɪnɪʃ〕v. 完成；做完（在此指「看完」）
  interesting〔ˈɪntrɪstɪŋ〕adj. 有趣的
  Really? 真的嗎？（尾音上揚）
  great〔gret〕adj. 很棒的　　**think of** 認為

26. (**C**) M：What would you like in your coffee?

W：Nothing. I take it black.

M：Really? I always add a lot of milk and sugar.

Question：What will the man drink?

A. Black coffee.

B. A glass of milk.

C. Coffee with milk and sugar.

* **What would you like in your coffee?** 你想要加什麼在
  咖啡裡？　　nothing〔ˈnʌθɪŋ〕pron. 什麼也沒有
  take〔tek〕v. 吃；喝
  black〔blæk〕adj. 不加牛奶或奶精的
  always〔ˈɔlwez〕adv. 總是　　add〔æd〕v. 添加
  milk〔mɪlk〕n. 牛奶　　sugar〔ˈʃugɚ〕n. 糖
  black coffee 黑咖啡（不加牛奶或奶精的咖啡）
  a glass of～ 一杯～

27. (**B**) M：Congratulations on winning the first prize.

W：Thank you. I was really surprised.

M：Why should you be surprised? You worked hard.

Question：What does the man mean?

A. He is surprised that the woman won.

B. The woman deserved to win.

C. The woman should have won, but she didn't.

* congratulations〔kən͵grætʃə'leʃəns〕 *interj.* 恭喜
win〔wɪn〕*v.* 贏得　　***first prize*** 頭獎
really〔'riəlɪ〕*adv.* 真地
surprised〔sə'praɪzd〕*adj.* 驚訝的
hard〔hard〕*adv.* 努力地　　deserve〔dɪ'zɝv〕*v.* 應得
mean〔min〕*v.* 意思是　　***should have + p.p.*** 早該～

28. (**A**) M：How much is this going to cost?

W：That depends on what's wrong with the car, sir.

M：When will you know?

W：As soon as I have a look at the engine.

Question：Who is the woman?

A. She is a mechanic.　　B. She is a driver.

C. She is an engineer.

* cost〔kɔst〕*v.* 值…（錢）
depends on ～　取決於～；視～而定
what's wrong with ～　～有什麼故障；～哪裡不對勁
as soon as 一…就～　　***have a look at*** ～　看一看～
engine〔'ɛndʒən〕*n.* 引擎　mechanic〔mə'kænɪk〕*n.* 技工
driver〔'draɪvɚ〕*n.* 駕駛人
engineer〔͵ɛndʒə'nɪr〕*n.* 工程師

29. (**B**) M：I'd like two dozen roses, please.

W：Would you like them delivered or do you want to take them with you?

M：Please deliver them to this address.

Question：Where did this conversation take place?

A. It is a delivery company.

B. In a flower shop.

C. She will deliver them to the address.

* ***would like*** 想要（＝ *want*）　　dozen〔'dʌzn̩〕*n.* 一打

rose〔roz〕*n.* 玫瑰　　deliver〔dɪ'lɪvɚ〕*v.* 遞送

address〔ə'drɛs, 'ædrɛs〕*n.* 地址

conversation〔͵kɑnvɚ'seʃən〕*n.* 對話

take place 發生　　delivery〔dɪ'lɪvərɪ〕*n.* 遞送

company〔'kʌmpənɪ〕*n.* 公司　　***flower shop*** 花店

30. (**C**) M：Can you hear me?

W：No. It's too noisy in here.

M：OK. Call me back when you get outside.

Question：Where are they talking?

A. They are outside.

B. They are too noisy.

C. They are talking on the phone.

* hear〔hɪr〕*v.* 聽見　　noisy〔'nɔɪzɪ〕*adj.* 吵鬧的

call sb. back 回某人電話

outside〔'aʊt'saɪd〕*adv.* 在外面

talk on the phone 講電話

全民英語能力分級檢定測驗
初級測驗⑧

　　本測驗分三部份，全為三選一之選擇題，每部份各 10 題，共 30 題，作答時間約 20 分鐘。

第一部份：看圖辨義

　　　　本部份共 10 題，試題冊上每題有一個圖片，請聽錄音機播出一個相關的問題，與 A、B、C 三個英語敘述後，選一個與所看到圖片最相符的答案，並在答案紙上相對的圓圈內塗黑作答。每題播出一遍，問題及選項均不印在試題冊上。

例：（看）

（聽）

Look at the picture.　How much is the hamburger?

　　A.　It's eighty dollars.
　　B.　It's fifty-five dollars.
　　C.　It's eighteen dollars.

正確答案為 A

Questions 1

Question 2

Questions 3

Question 4

Question 5

請翻頁 ▯⟹

<u>Question 6</u>

<u>Question 7</u>

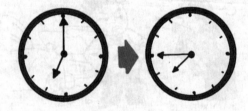

<u>Question 8</u>

Question 9

Question 10

第二部份：問答

本部份共 10 題，每題錄音機會播出一個問句或直述句，每題播出一次，聽後請從試題冊上 A、B、C 三個選項中，選出一個最適合的回答或回應，並在答案紙上塗黑作答。

例：

（聽） Good morning, Kevin. How are you?

（看） A. I'm fine, thank you.
B. I'm in the living room.
C. My name is Kevin.

正確答案為 A

11. A. Last year.
B. In elementary school.
C. Central High School.

12. A. Every day except Sunday.
B. At 9:30.
C. Last September.

13. A. Yes. A size 36, please.
B. Thank you, but they are already tied.
C. Cash or charge?

14. A. No, thanks. We're fine.
B. Don't worry. I brought it.
C. Where did you get it?

15. A. I read every day.
    B. I'm up to page 80.
    C. Yes, I have.

16. A. That would be nice.
    B. Be careful. The
       water is deep.
    C. No, I don't like
       driving.

17. A. Of course I like
       her.
    B. Not at all.
    C. There she is!

18. A. We all have six classes
       a day.
    B. There are forty-two.
    C. Yes, I have many
       classmates.

19. A. You can leave it open
       until six o'clock.
    B. Yes, you may.
    C. It's locked. Use the key.

20. A. How do you do?
    B. No, the meeting is at
       three.
    C. I don't think so.

請 翻 頁

第三部份： 簡短對話

本部份共 10 題，每題錄音機會播出一段對話及一個相關的問題，每題播出兩次，聽後請從試題冊上 A、B、C 三個選項中，選出一個最適合的回答，並在答案紙上塗黑作答。

例：

(聽) (Woman) Good afternoon, …Mr. Davis?

(Man) Yes. I have an appointment with Dr. Sanders at two o'clock. My son Tommy has a fever.

(Woman) Oh, that's too bad. Well, please have a seat, Mr. Davis. Dr. Sanders will be right with you.

Question: Where did this conversation take place?

(看) A. In a post office.
B. In a restaurant.
C. In a doctor's office.

正確答案為 C

21. A. She will fail if she is too nervous.
    B. She will have to take the class again.
    C. She will not do well in class.

22. A. They are watching television.
    B. They are knocking on the door.
    C. They are listening to the sounds of nature.

23. A. She is the manager.
    B. Wait for the manager.
    C. Ask for help.

24. A. The army.
    B. To go to school.
    C. Three years ago.

25. A. Something to eat for dinner.
    B. Around twenty people.
    C. A bottle of wine.

請 翻 頁

26. A. His house was too
       old.
    B. He wanted to live in
       a smaller place.
    C. His apartment was
       too expensive for him.

27. A. He forgot what time
       it will start.
    B. He has to go out with
       the woman.
    C. He cannot find the
       TV schedule.

28. A. Because she slept too
       late.
    B. She forgot to do it.
    C. She ate nothing.

29. A. He hurt his finger
       playing volleyball.
    B. He played too
       soon and hurt his
       finger.
    C. He broke his finger.

30. A. The man usually
       catches a cold in
       the winter.
    B. The woman is
       usually cold.
    C. The woman often
       gets sick in the
       summer.

初級英語聽力檢定⑧詳解

第一部份

Look at the picture for question 1.

1. (**C**) Where is the jewelry?
   A. The woman is stealing it.
   B. The salesclerk.   C. On the counter.

   * jewelry〔'dʒuəlrɪ〕 n. 珠寶
     steal〔stil〕 v. 偷（三態變化為：steal-stole-stolen）
     salesclerk〔'selz,klɜk〕 n. 售貨員
     counter〔'kaʊntə〕 n. 櫃台

Look at the picture for question 2.

2. (**B**) What is the man saying?
   A. To the crowd.   B. He is making a speech.
   C. On the stage.

   * crowd〔kraʊd〕 n. 群眾
     make a speech 發表演說   stage〔stedʒ〕 n. 舞台

Look at the picture for question 3.

3. (**B**) Who is the man?
   A. Is this seat taken?   B. He is a customer.
   C. He has a hamburger.

   * take〔tek〕 v. 佔（位子）
     Is this seat taken? 這個位子有人坐嗎？
     customer〔'kʌstəmə〕 n. 顧客
     hamburger〔'hæmbɜgə〕 n. 漢堡

Look at the picture for question 4.

4. (**A**)　What are they doing?

　　A. They are arguing.

　　B. They are crashing.

　　C. They are damaged.

　　＊ argue〔'ɑrgjʊ〕v. 爭論　　crash〔kræʃ〕v.（車子）相撞
　　　　damage〔'dæmɪdʒ〕v. 損害

Look at the picture for question 5.

5. (**B**)　What is happening?

　　A. How do you do?

　　B. An introduction.

　　C. They are dancing.

　　＊ happen〔'hæpən〕v. 發生
　　　　How do you do? 你好嗎？（初次見面的問候語）
　　　　introduction〔ˌɪntrə'dʌkʃən〕n. 介紹
　　　　dance〔dæns〕v. 跳舞

Look at the picture for question 6.

6. (**B**)　Which word describes her?

　　A. Scale.　　　　　　B. Overweight.

　　C. Diet.

　　＊ which〔hwɪtʃ〕adj. 哪一個
　　　　describe〔dɪ'skraɪb〕v. 描述　　scale〔skel〕n. 磅秤
　　　　overweight〔'ovɚ'wet〕adj. 過重的
　　　　diet〔'daɪət〕n. 飲食；節食

Look at the picture for question 7.

7. (**C**) How much time has passed?

    A. It is past seven.

    B. A quarter.

    C. Forty-five minutes.

    * pass〔pæs〕*v.* 經過

    past〔pæst〕*prep.* (時間) 超過

    quarter〔'kwɔrtɚ〕*n.* 十五分鐘;一刻鐘

Look at the picture for question 8.

8. (**B**) What is on the paper?

    A. A boy.

    B. A mountain.

    C. A table.

    * paper〔'pepɚ〕*n.* 紙   mountain〔'mauntn̩〕*n.* 山

    table〔'tebl̩〕*n.* 桌子

Look at the picture for question 9.

9. (**B**) What is outside?

    A. It is cloudy.

    B. Clothes.

    C. They are drying.

    * outside〔'aut'saɪd〕*adv.* 在外面

    cloudy〔'klaudɪ〕*adj.* 多雲的

    clothes〔kloðz〕*n. pl.* 衣服

    dry〔draɪ〕*v.* 曬乾;變乾

Look at the picture for question 10.

10. (**C**) Which is the most expensive fruit?

    A. NT$30.

    B. None of them.

    C. Watermelon.

    * which〔hwɪtʃ〕*pron.* 哪一個

      expensive〔ɪk'spɛnsɪv〕*adj.* 昂貴的

      fruit〔frut〕*n.* 水果   *none of~* ~其中都沒有

      watermelon〔'wɔtə‚mɛlən〕*n.* 西瓜

第二部份

11. (**C**) Where did you go to school?

    A. Last year.

    B. In elementary school.

    C. Central High School.

    * elementary〔‚ɛlə'mɛntərɪ〕*adj.* 初等的

      elementary school 小學

      central〔'sɛntrəl〕*adj.* 中央的   *high school* 高中

12. (**B**) What time do you open?

    A. Every day except Sunday.

    B. At 9:30.

    C. Last September.

    * *what time* 幾點   open〔'opən〕*v.* (開門) 營業

      except〔ɪk'sɛpt〕*prep.* 除了⋯之外

      last September 去年九月

13. (**A**) Would you like to try those shoes on?

    A. Yes. A size 36, please.

    B. Thank you, but they are already tied.

    C. Cash or charge?

    * **Would you like to V.～?** 你想要～嗎？
    try on 試穿   shoes〔ʃuz〕*n. pl.* 鞋子
    already〔ɔl'rɛdɪ〕*adv.* 已經   tie〔taɪ〕*v.* 綁
    cash〔kæʃ〕*n.* 現金
    charge〔tʃɑrdʒ〕*v.* 把消費記帳上
    Cash or charge? 付現還是刷卡？

14. (**A**) Can I bring you anything else?

    A. No, thanks. We're fine.

    B. Don't worry. I brought it.

    C. Where did you get it?

    * bring〔brɪŋ〕*v.* 帶（東西）給（人）
    else〔ɛls〕*adj.* 別的；其他的
    fine〔faɪn〕*adj.* 沒問題的；很好的
    worry〔'wɜɪ〕*v.* 擔心   get〔gɛt〕*v.* 買

15. (**B**) How much of the reading have you done?

    A. I read every day.

    B. I'm up to page 80.

    C. Yes, I have.

    * reading〔'ridɪŋ〕*n.* 閱讀   do〔du〕*v.* 完成；做完
    up to 達到   page〔pedʒ〕*n.* 頁

16. (**A**) Would you like me to drive?

    A. That would be nice.

    B. Be careful. The water is deep.

    C. No, I don't like driving.

    * drive〔draɪv〕*v.* 開車　　nice〔naɪs〕*adj.* 好的
    Be careful. 小心。　　deep〔dip〕*adj.* 深的

17. (**B**) Do you look like your sister?

    A. Of course I like her.

    B. Not at all.　　　C. There she is!

    * ***look like*** ~ 看起來像~　　like〔laɪk〕*v.* 喜歡
    Not at all. 一點也不。（ 在此指「完全不像。」）
    There she is! 她來了；她就在那裡！

18. (**B**) How many students are there in your class?

    A. We all have six classes a day.

    B. There are forty-two.

    C. Yes, I have many classmates.

    * class〔klæs〕*n.* 班；課
    classmate〔'klæs,met〕*n.* 同班同學

19. (**C**) How can I open this door?

    A. You can leave it open until six o'clock.

    B. Yes, you may.

    C. It's locked. Use the key.

    * open〔'opən〕*v.* 打開　　leave〔liv〕*v.* 使（維持在某種狀態）
    may〔me〕*aux.* 可以　　lock〔lɑk〕*v.* 鎖住
    use〔juz〕*v.* 使用

20. (**C**) Have we met before?

    A. How do you do?

    B. No, the meeting is at three.

    C. I don't think so.

    * meet〔mit〕v. 相遇；見面　　before〔bɪˋfor〕adv. 以前
    meeting〔ˋmitɪŋ〕n. 會議
    I don't think so. 我想不是；我不這麼認為。

第三部份

21. (**B**) M：Why are you so worried about this exam?

    W：If I don't do well, I can't advance to the next class.

    M：You always do well in class. I'm sure you'll pass.

    W：Yes, but I get nervous during tests.

    Question：What will happen if the woman fails?

    A. She will fail if she is too nervous.

    B. She will have to take the class again.

    C. She will not do well in class.

    * ***be worried about*** 擔心
    exam〔ɪgˋzæm〕n. 考試（= *examination*〔ɪgˌzæməˋneʃən〕）
    do well 考得好　　advance〔ədˋvæns〕v. 升級；晉升
    class〔klæs〕n. 班；年級　　always〔ˋɔlwez〕adv. 總是
    sure〔ʃur〕adj. 確信的　　pass〔pæs〕v. 及格
    get〔gɛt〕v. 變得　　nervous〔ˋnɝvəs〕adj. 緊張的
    during〔ˋdjurɪŋ〕prep. 在…期間　　test〔tɛst〕n. 考試
    happen〔ˋhæpən〕v. 發生　　fail〔fel〕v. 不及格
    have to 必須　　take〔tek〕v. 修（課）

22. (**A**) M：Did you hear that?

W：What?

M：It sounded like a knock on the door.

W：I think it was the TV.

Question：What are they doing?

A. They are watching television.

B. They are knocking on the door.

C. They are listening to the sounds of nature.

* hear〔hɪr〕*v.* 聽見　　***sound like*** 聽起來像

knock〔nɑk〕*n.* 敲門聲　*v.* 敲　　think〔θɪŋk〕*v.* 認為

watch〔wɑtʃ〕*v.* 看（電視）

television〔'tɛləˌvɪʒən〕*n.* 電視　　***listen to*** 傾聽

nature〔'netʃɚ〕*n.* 大自然

23. (**C**) M：Do you know where I can find a box of half-inch nails?

W：No, I don't.　But I can ask the manager.

M：Thanks.　I'll wait.

Question：What will the woman do?

A. She is the manager.

B. Wait for the manager.

C. Ask for help.

* find〔faɪnd〕*v.* 找到　　half-inch〔ˌhæf'ɪntʃ〕*adj.* 半吋的

nail〔nel〕*n.* 釘子　　ask〔æsk〕*v.* 問；請求

manager〔'mænɪdʒɚ〕*n.* 經理　　wait〔wet〕*v.* 等

help〔hɛlp〕*n.* 幫助

24. (**A**) M：Were you ever in the military?

W：Yes. I spent three years in the army.

M：Why did you leave it?

W：I wanted to go back to school.

Question：What did the woman leave?

A. The army. B. To go to school.

C. Three years ago.

* ever〔'ɛvɚ〕*adv.* 曾經　　military〔'mɪlə,tɛrɪ〕*n.* 軍隊
spend〔spɛnd〕*v.* 度過（時間）
army〔'ɑrmɪ〕*n.* 陸軍　　leave〔liv〕*v.* 離開
go back to 回到　　ago〔ə'go〕*adv.* …以前

25. (**C**) M：How many people will be at the party?

W：Oh, around twenty.

M：That's a lot.

W：Not really. I'm not serving dinner —— just drinks
and some snacks.

M：Can I bring anything?

Question：What might the man bring to the party?

A. Something to eat for dinner.

B. Around twenty people.

C. A bottle of wine.

* around〔ə'raʊnd〕*adv.* 大約　　*Not really.* 倒也不見得。
serve〔sɝv〕*v.* 供應　　drink〔drɪŋk〕*n.* 飲料
snack〔snæk〕*n.* 點心　　might〔maɪt〕*aux.* 可能
a bottle of～ 一瓶～　　wine〔waɪn〕*n.* 酒；葡萄酒

26. (**C**) M：Why did Ted move?

W：His rent went up and he couldn't afford it.

M：Did he move to a smaller place?

W：Yeah, it's about half the size of his old one, but it's a lot cheaper.

Question：Why did Ted move?

A. His house was too old.

B. He wanted to live in a smaller place.

C. His apartment was too expensive for him.

* move〔muv〕v. 搬家　　rent〔rɛnt〕n. 房租

go up 上升；上漲　　afford〔ə'fɔrd〕v. 負擔得起

smaller〔'smɔlə〕adj. 較小的（small 的比較級）

place〔ples〕n. 地方

yeah〔jæ, jɛ〕adv. 是的（= yes）

about〔ə'baʊt〕adv. 大約

half the size of~　~的一半大小

a lot cheaper 便宜很多　　old〔old〕adj. 老舊的

apartment〔ə'pɑrtmənt〕n. 公寓

27. (**B**) M：Have you seen the TV schedule?

W：No. Why?

M：I want to know what time the game starts.

W：You can't watch the game. We're going out tonight.

M：Oh! I forgot.

Question：Why can't the man watch the game?

A. He forgot what time it will start.

B. He has to go out with the woman.

C. He cannot find the TV schedule.

* schedule〔'skɛdʒul〕*n.* 時間表　***TV schedule*** 電視節目表
game〔gem〕*n.* 比賽　　start〔stɑrt〕*v.* 開始
go out 外出　　tonight〔tə'naɪt〕*adv.* 今晚
oh〔o〕*interj.* 喔（因驚訝所發出的感嘆）
forget〔fɚ'gɛt〕*v.* 忘記

28. (**C**)　M：Did you have breakfast?

W：No. I didn't have time.

M：Why not?

W：I forgot to set my alarm.

Question：What did the woman have for breakfast?

A. Because she slept too late.

B. She forgot to do it.　　C. She ate nothing.

* have〔hæv〕*v.* 吃　　breakfast〔'brɛkfəst〕*n.* 早餐
Why not? 爲什麼沒時間？　　set〔sɛt〕*v.* 設定
alarm〔ə'lɑrm〕*n.* 鬧鐘　　because〔bɪ'kɔz〕*prep.* 因爲
sleep〔slip〕*v.* 睡覺　　late〔let〕*adv.* 晚
nothing〔'nʌθɪŋ〕*pron.* 什麼也沒有

29. (**A**)　M：Is it broken, doctor?

W：No. But you won't be able to play volleyball for a
while.

M：Oh, no! The championship is next week!

W：I'm sorry. But if you play too soon, you will hurt
your finger again.

Question：Why can't the man play in the championship game?

A. He hurt his finger playing volleyball.

B. He played too soon and hurt his finger.

C. He broke his finger.

* broken〔'brokən〕*adj.* 斷了的　　***be able to V.*** 能夠～
play〔ple〕*v.* 打（球）　　volleyball〔'vɑlɪ,bɔl〕*n.* 排球
for a while （持續）一段時間
championship〔'tʃæmpɪən,ʃɪp〕*n.* 冠軍賽
soon〔sun〕*adv.* 早；很快地　　hurt〔hɜt〕*v.* 使受傷
finger〔'fɪŋɡɚ〕*n.* 手指　　again〔ə'ɡɛn〕*adv.* 再一次
break〔brek〕*v.* 折斷

30. (**C**)　M：Do you often catch cold?

W：Yes.　I usually catch a cold in the summer.

M：That's strange.　I usually get colds in the winter.

Question：What is strange?

A. The man usually catches a cold in the winter.

B. The woman is usually cold.

C. The woman often gets sick in the summer.

* often〔'ɔfən〕*adv.* 經常
cold〔kold〕*n.* 感冒　*adj.* 冷的
catch cold 感冒（= *catch a cold*）
usually〔'juʒʊəlɪ〕*adv.* 通常　　summer〔'sʌmɚ〕*n.* 夏天
strange〔strendʒ〕*adj.* 奇怪的　　get〔ɡɛt〕*v.* 患（病）
winter〔'wɪntɚ〕*n.* 冬天　　sick〔sɪk〕*adj.* 生病的

全民英語能力分級檢定測驗
初級測驗⑨

本測驗分三部份，全為三選一之選擇題，每部份各 10 題，共 30 題，作答時間約 20 分鐘。

第一部份：看圖辨義

　　　　　本部份共 10 題，試題冊上每題有一個圖片，請聽錄音機播出一個相關的問題，與 A、B、C 三個英語敘述後，選一個與所看到圖片最相符的答案，並在答案紙上相對的圓圈內塗黑作答。每題播出一遍，問題及選項均不印在試題冊上。

例：（看）

（聽）

Look at the picture.　How much is the hamburger?

　　A. It's eighty dollars.
　　B. It's fifty-five dollars.
　　C. It's eighteen dollars.

正確答案為 A

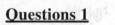

Questions 1

Question 2

Questions 3

Question 4

Question 5

請 翻 頁 ◀▢▢◀━━▷

Question 6

Question 7

Question 8

Question 9

Question 10

請翻頁 ⟹

第二部份： 問答

本部份共 10 題，每題錄音機會播出一個問句或直述句，
每題播出一次，聽後請從試題冊上 A、B、C 三個選項
中，選出一個最適合的回答或回應，並在答案紙上塗黑
作答。

例：

（聽）　Good morning, Kevin. How are you?

（看）　A.　I'm fine, thank you.
　　　　B.　I'm in the living room.
　　　　C.　My name is Kevin.

正確答案爲 A

11. A. It's on Elm Street.
　　B. That's the high school.
　　C. No, it's that one over
　　　　there.

12. A. Yes, I did.
　　B. What's your number?
　　C. Of course I will.

13. A. You're welcome.
　　B. Yes, I have it.
　　C. How much is it?

14. A. How much was it?
　　B. I have two liters.
　　C. No, it's too deep.

15. A. Sure. What do you
    need?
    B. There it is.
    C. No. I will continue
    to go there.

16. A. It's a beautiful color.
    B. What a lovely
    picture!
    C. Where did you get it?

17. A. Congratulations!
    B. Don't worry. It can
    be repaired.
    C. It's under your desk.

18. A. I often walk my dog
    in the park.
    B. Yes, I have two
    dogs.
    C. No, that's not him.

19. A. It has a flat tire.
    B. Yes, I'm very happy
    with it.
    C. It's a Toyota.

20. A. It's only 500 dollars.
    B. The one on First
    Street.
    C. The blue sweater.

請 翻 頁 ◀▭⟹

第三部份：　簡短對話

　　　　本部份共 10 題，每題錄音機會播出一段對話及一個相關
的問題，每題播出兩次，聽後請從試題冊上 A、B、C 三
個選項中，選出一個最適合的回答，並在答案紙上塗黑
作答。

例：

(聽)　(Woman)　Good afternoon, …Mr. Davis?

　　　(Man)　　　Yes.　I have an appointment with
　　　　　　　　Dr. Sanders at two o'clock.　My
　　　　　　　　son Tommy has a fever.

　　　(Woman)　Oh, that's too bad.　Well, please
　　　　　　　　have a seat, Mr. Davis.　Dr.
　　　　　　　　Sanders will be right with you.

　　　Question:　Where did this conversation take
　　　　　　　　place?

(看)　A.　In a post office.

　　　B.　In a restaurant.

　　　C.　In a doctor's office.

　　　　正確答案爲 C

21. A. A new form.
    B. A pen.
    C. A pencil.

22. A. The cold weather.
    B. Sue's absence.
    C. Sue's work.

23. A. They will see it at a different movie theater.
    B. They will watch *Star Wars* on a different day.
    C. They will watch a different movie.

24. A. What her job is.
    B. How she feels.
    C. Why she came to Taipei.

25. A. He ordered it last week.
    B. He wanted to give it to his son.
    C. His son was very disappointed.

26. A. He will deliver a pizza.
    B. He will make a pizza.
    C. He will call a pizza shop.

請 翻 頁 ⇒

27. A. He wants to give the
woman a driving test.
   B. He wants to celebrate
the woman's passing
the test.
   C. He wants to see the
woman's driver's
license.

28. A. The man lost it.
   B. It is missing.
   C. Someone checked it
out of the library.

29. A. The man looks the
same as he did five
years ago.
   B. Most people will
look different after
five years.
   C. The man doesn't look
the same and neither
does anyone else.

30. A. Ten percent.
   B. 1000 dollars.
   C. 900 dollars.

初級英語聽力檢定 ⑨ 詳解

第一部份

Look at the picture for question 1.

1. (**A**) What did the woman do?

      A. She set the table.   B. She is a waitress.

      C. She is hungry.

    * ***set the table*** 擺放餐具

      waitress〔'wetrɪs〕*n.* 女服務生

      hungry〔'hʌŋgrɪ〕*adj.* 飢餓的

Look at the picture for question 2.

2. (**B**) Why did the man fall down?

      A. He was on the stairs.

      B. He was reading while walking.

      C. He lost his glasses.

    * ***fall down*** 跌倒   stairs〔stɛrz〕*n. pl.* 樓梯

      while〔hwaɪl〕*conj.* 當⋯的時候   walk〔wɔk〕*v.* 走路

      lose〔luz〕*v.* 遺失   glasses〔'glæsɪz〕*n. pl.* 眼鏡

Look at the picture for question 3.

3. (**B**) What is the man on the left doing?

      A. He is shaking.

      B. He is robbing someone.

      C. He is asking for help.

    * left〔lɛft〕*n.* 左邊   shake〔ʃek〕*v.* 發抖

      rob〔rɑb〕*v.* 搶劫   ***ask for*** 請求   help〔hɛlp〕*n.* 幫助

Look at the picture for question 4.

4. (**C**) Does the girl feel bad?

    A. Yes, it does.

    B. Because her hair is wet.

    C. Yes. Her head aches.

    * *feel bad* 覺得不舒服　　because〔bɪˈkɔz〕*conj.* 因為

    hair〔hɛr〕*n.* 頭髮　　wet〔wɛt〕*adj.* 濕的

    head〔hɛd〕*n.* 頭　　ache〔ek〕*v.* 疼痛

Look at the picture for question 5.

5. (**C**) What does the customer want?

    A. A post office.

    B. At window number three.

    C. An envelope.

    * customer〔ˈkʌstəmɚ〕*n.* 顧客　　*post office* 郵局

    window〔ˈwɪndo〕*n.*（郵局、售票等）窗口

    number〔ˈnʌmbɚ〕*n.* 第～號

    envelope〔ˈɛnvəˌlop〕*n.* 信封

Look at the picture for question 6.

6. (**C**) What are the children carrying?

    A. Boots.

    B. Jackets.

    C. Umbrellas.

    * children〔ˈtʃɪldrən〕*n. pl.* 小孩（單數為 child）

    carry〔ˈkærɪ〕*v.* 攜帶　　boots〔buts〕*n. pl.* 靴子

    jacket〔ˈdʒækɪt〕*n.* 夾克　　umbrella〔ʌmˈbrɛlə〕*n.* 雨傘

Look at the picture for question 7.

7. (**A**) What happened while the woman was talking?
   A. The soup boiled.
   B. The phone rang.
   C. It was not long enough.

   * happen〔'hæpən〕*v.* 發生
     while〔hwaɪl〕*conj.* 當…的時候
     soup〔sup〕*n.* 湯　　boil〔bɔɪl〕*v.* 沸騰
     phone〔fon〕*n.* 電話 (= *telephone*)
     ring〔rɪŋ〕*v.* (鈴) 響 (三態變化爲：ring-rang-rung)
     enough〔ə'nʌf〕*adv.* 足夠地

Look at the picture for question 8.

8. (**B**) Where is the boy?
   A. He wants a cake.
   B. Outside a bakery.
   C. It is delicious.

   * cake〔kck〕*n.* 蛋糕
     outside〔'aʊt'saɪd〕*prep.* 在…外面
     bakery〔'bekərɪ〕*n.* 麵包店
     delicious〔dɪ'lɪʃəs〕*adj.* 美味的

Look at the picture for question 9.

9. (**B**) Which book is on the bottom?

    A. There are four.

    B. The largest.

    C. It is lighter.

    * which〔hwɪtʃ〕*adv.* 哪一個　　bottom〔'bɑtəm〕*n.* 底部

    largest〔'lɑrdʒɪst〕*adj.* 最大的 (large 的最高級)

    lighter〔'laɪtɚ〕*adj.* 較輕的 (light 的比較級)

Look at the picture for question 10.

10. (**B**) Is English Pat's favorite subject?

    A. Yes, he is studying English.

    B. No, it's not.

    C. England is his favorite.

    * favorite〔'fevərɪt〕*adj.* 最喜愛的　*n.* 最喜愛的人或物

    subject〔'sʌbdʒɪkt〕*n.* 科目

    England〔'ɪŋglənd〕*n.* 英國

第二部份

11. (**B**) What's that building over there?

    A. It's on Elm Street.

    B. That's the high school.

    C. No, it's that one over there.

    * building〔'bɪldɪŋ〕*n.* 建築物；大樓

    over there 在那裡　　street〔strit〕*n.* 街道

    high school 高中

12. (**A**)　Did you just call me?

　　　A.　Yes, I did.

　　　B.　What's your number?

　　　C.　Of course I will.

　　　* just〔dʒʌst〕*adv.* 剛剛

　　　　number〔'nʌmbɚ〕*n.* 電話號碼　　*of course* 當然

13. (**C**)　Here is that book you asked for.

　　　A.　You're welcome.

　　　B.　Yes, I have it.

　　　C.　How much is it?

　　　* *Here is* ～. 這是～。　　*ask for* 要求

　　　　You're welcome. 不客氣。

14. (**B**)　Did you remember to bring enough water?

　　　A.　How much was it?

　　　B.　I have two liters.

　　　C.　No, it's too deep.

　　　* remember〔rɪ'mɛmbɚ〕*v.* 記得

　　　　bring〔brɪŋ〕*v.* 帶來

　　　　enough〔ə'nʌf〕*adj.* 足夠的

　　　　liter〔'litɚ〕*n.* 公升　　deep〔dip〕*adj.* 深的

15. (**A**) Can you stop by the store on your way home?

    A. Sure. What do you need?

    B. There it is.

    C. No. I will continue to go there.

    * ***stop by***~ 途中順便停留在~

    on your way home 在你回家途中

    sure〔 ʃʊr 〕*adv.* 好；當然   need〔 nid 〕*v.* 需要

    There it is. 就在那裡。   continue〔 kən'tɪnju 〕*v.* 繼續

16. (**B**) And this is my niece.

    A. It's a beautiful color.

    B. What a lovely picture!

    C. Where did you get it?

    * niece〔 nis 〕*n.* 姪女；外甥女   color〔'kʌlə 〕*n.* 顏色

    lovely〔'lʌvlɪ 〕*adj.* 可愛的；美麗的

    picture〔'pɪktʃə 〕*n.* 相片   get〔 gɛt 〕*v.* 買；得到

17. (**C**) My bag is missing!

    A. Congratulations!

    B. Don't worry. It can be repaired.

    C. It's under your desk.

    * bag〔 bæg 〕*n.* 袋子

    missing〔'mɪsɪŋ 〕*adj.* 失蹤的；找不到的

    congratulations〔 kən͵grætʃə'leʃənz 〕*interj.* 恭喜

    worry〔'wɝɪ 〕*v.* 擔心   repair〔 rɪ'pɛr 〕*v.* 修理

    under〔'ʌndə 〕*prep.* 在…之下   desk〔 dɛsk 〕*n.* 書桌

18. (**C**) Is that your dog running in the park?

    A. I often walk my dog in the park.

    B. Yes, I have two dogs.

    C. No, that's not him.

    * run〔rʌn〕v. 跑   park〔pɑrk〕n. 公園

    often〔'ɔfən〕adv. 經常   walk〔wɔk〕v. 遛（狗）

19. (**A**) What happened to your car?

    A. It has a flat tire.

    B. Yes, I'm very happy with it.

    C. It's a Toyota.

    * happen〔'hæpən〕v. 發生

    flat〔flæt〕adj. （輪胎）沒氣的

    tire〔taɪr〕n. 輪胎   **be happy with**～ 對～感到滿意

    Toyota 豐田汽車（日本汽車品牌）

20. (**B**) Which store is cheaper?

    A. It's only 500 dollars.

    B. The one on First Street.

    C. The blue sweater.

    * which〔hwɪtʃ〕adj. 哪一個   store〔stor〕n. 商店

    cheaper〔'tʃipɚ〕adj. 較便宜的（cheap 的比較級）

    only〔'onlɪ〕adv. 只有   dollar〔'dɑlɚ〕n. 元

    First Street 第一街（街名）

    blue〔blu〕adj. 藍色的   sweater〔'swɛtɚ〕n. 毛衣

第三部份

21. (**B**)　M：I'm sorry, but you'll have to fill out this form again.

W：Did I make a mistake?

M：You have to use a blue or black pen, not a pencil.

W：Oh, sorry.　Can I borrow one?

M：Here you are.

Question：What did the woman borrow?

A. A new form.

B. A pen.

C. A pencil.

* ***have to*** 必須　　***fill out*** 填寫

form〔fɔrm〕*n.* 表格　　again〔ə'gɛn〕*adv.* 再一次

make a mistake 犯錯　　use〔juz〕*v.* 使用

black〔blæk〕*adj.* 黑色的

pen〔pɛn〕*n.* 筆（原子筆、鋼筆等）

pencil〔'pɛnsḷ〕*n.* 鉛筆

borrow〔'baro〕*v.* 借（入）

Here you are. 你要的東西在這裡；拿去吧。（= *Here it is.*）

22. (**B**)　M：What's the matter with Sue?

W：She has a bad cold.

M：When will she come back to work?

W：Next week, I think.

Question：What are they discussing?

A. The cold weather.

B. Sue's absence.

C. Sue's work.

* ***What's the matter with sb.?*** 某人怎麼了？
cold〔kold〕*n.* 感冒　*adj.* 寒冷的
bad〔bæd〕*adj.* 嚴重的　***have a bad cold*** 得了重感冒
come back 回來　　think〔θɪŋk〕*v.* 認為；想
discuss〔dɪ'skʌs〕*v.* 討論　　weather〔'wɛðɚ〕*n.* 天氣
absence〔'æbsn̩s〕*n.* 缺席

23. (**C**) M：What a long line!

W：Yeah. I guess everyone had the same idea.

M：I hope we can get tickets.

W：If we can't get tickets for *Star Wars*, we can always
see a different movie.

Question：What will they do if they cannot get tickets
for *Star Wars*?

A. They will see it at a different movie theater.

B. They will watch *Star Wars* on a different day.

C. They will watch a different movie.

* line〔laɪn〕*n.* 隊伍　***What a long line!*** 好長的隊伍啊！
yeah〔jæ, jɛ〕*adv.* 是的（= *yes*）　　guess〔gɛs〕*v.* 猜想
same〔sem〕*adj.* 相同的　　idea〔aɪ'diə〕*n.* 想法
hope〔hop〕*v.* 希望　　get〔gɛt〕*v.* 買到
ticket〔'tɪkɪt〕*n.* 票　　***Star Wars*** 星際大戰（電影名）
different〔'dɪfərənt〕*adj.* 不同的
movie theater 電影院

24. (**A**) M: Do you live around here?

W: No. I'm from Taichung. I came to Taipei for a meeting.

M: What do you do?

W: I sell computers.

Question: What did the man ask the woman?

A. What her job is.　　B. How she feels.

C. Why she came to Taipei.

* live〔lɪv〕v. 住　　around〔ə'raʊnd〕adv. 在⋯附近
Taichung〔'taɪ'tʃʊŋ〕n. 台中　　meeting〔'mitɪŋ〕n. 會議
What do you do? 你的職業是什麼？
sell〔sɛl〕v. 賣；銷售　　computer〔kəm'pjutɚ〕n. 電腦
job〔dʒɑb〕n. 工作；職業　　feel〔fil〕v. 覺得

25. (**B**) M: Do you have the new *Harry Potter* book?

W: I'm sorry, sir. I sold the last one yesterday.

M: Oh, no! My son will be very disappointed.

W: I can order one for you and it will be here next week.

M: But his birthday is tomorrow.

Question: Why did the man want the *Harry Potter* book?

A. He ordered it last week.

B. He wanted to give it to his son.

C. His son was very disappointed.

* ***Harry Potter*** 哈利波特（小說名）
last〔læst〕adj. 最後的　　son〔sʌn〕n. 兒子
disappointed〔‚dɪsə'pɔɪntɪd〕adj. 失望的
order〔'ɔrdɚ〕v. 訂購　　birthday〔'bɝθ‚de〕n. 生日

26. (**C**)　M：Do you know how to make pizza?

　　　　　W：Yes, but it's a lot easier to order one.

　　　　　M：OK.　I'll have one delivered.

　　　　　Question：What will the man do?

　　　　　A.　He will deliver a pizza.

　　　　　B.　He will make a pizza.

　　　　　C.　He will call a pizza shop.

　　　＊ make〔mek〕*v.* 做　　pizza〔'pitsə〕*n.* 披薩

　　　a lot easier 容易很多　　order〔'ɔrdɚ〕*v.* 點（菜）；訂購

　　　OK. 好的；沒問題　　deliver〔dɪ'lɪvɚ〕*v.* 遞送

　　　call〔kɔl〕*v.* 打電話給～　　shop〔ʃɑp〕*n.* 商店

27. (**B**)　M：Did you pass your driving test?

　　　　　W：Yes.　Here is my license.

　　　　　M：Congratulations!　Let's go for a drive.

　　　　　Question：What does the man want to do?

　　　　　A.　He wants to give the woman a driving test.

　　　　　B.　He wants to celebrate the woman's passing the test.

　　　　　C.　He wants to see the woman's driver's license.

　　　＊ pass〔pæs〕*v.* 通過（考試）

　　　driving〔'draɪvɪŋ〕*n.* 駕駛

　　　test〔tɛst〕*n.* 測驗　　**Here is ～.** 這是～。

　　　license〔'laɪsn̩s〕*n.* 執照（在此指 driver's license「駕照」）

　　　congratulations〔kən،grætʃə'leʃənz〕*interj.* 恭喜

　　　go for a drive 開車去兜風

　　　celebrate〔'sɛlə،bret〕*v.* 慶祝

28. (**B**)　M：I can't find the book I need.

　　　　　W：Hmm.　According to the computer, it's still in the library.

　　　　　M：But it's not on the shelf where it's supposed to be.

　　　　　W：Maybe somebody used it and put it back in the wrong place.

　　　Question：What happened to the book?

　　　A.　The man lost it.

　　　B.　It is missing.

　　　C.　Someone checked it out of the library.

　　　* find〔faɪnd〕v. 找到　　need〔nid〕v. 需要
　　　　hmm〔m, hm〕interj. 嗯；唔（= h'm）（思考或想引人注
　　　　　意時發出的聲音，聲音拉得越長，m 越多。）
　　　　according to 根據　　still〔stɪl〕adv. 仍然
　　　　library〔'laɪ,brɛrɪ〕n. 圖書館
　　　　shelf〔ʃɛlf〕n. 架子　　***be supposed to*** ~ 應該~
　　　　maybe〔'mebi〕adv. 也許
　　　　somebody〔'sʌm,bɑdɪ〕pron. 某人
　　　　use〔juz〕v. 使用　　put〔pʊt〕v. 放
　　　　back〔bæk〕adv. 返回　　wrong〔rɔŋ〕adj. 錯誤的
　　　　place〔ples〕n. 地方
　　　　happen〔'hæpən〕v. 發生　　lose〔luz〕v. 遺失
　　　　missing〔'mɪsɪŋ〕adj. 失蹤的；找不到的
　　　　library〔'laɪ,brɛrɪ〕n. 圖書館
　　　　check out （在圖書館）辦理借（書）的手續
　　　　check~out of the library 從圖書館借走~

29. (**A**) M：Are you going to the class reunion?

W：Of course. It will be fun to see everyone again after five years.

M：Yeah. I wonder if they will all look the same?

W：Well, you haven't changed.

Question：What does the woman mean?

A. The man looks the same as he did five years ago.

B. Most people will look different after five years.

C. The man doesn't look the same and neither does anyone else.

* reunion〔ri'junjən〕n. 重聚；團圓

class reunion 同學會　　*of course* 當然

fun〔fʌn〕adj. 好玩的；有趣的

yeah〔jæ, jɛ〕adv. 是的（= yes）

wonder〔'wʌndɚ〕v. 想知道

wonder if~ 不知是否

look〔luk〕v. 看起來　　*the same* 相同的

well〔wɛl〕interj. 那麼（用於繼續話題時）

change〔tʃendʒ〕v. 改變　　mean〔min〕v. 意思是

the same as~ 與~相同的

neither〔'niðɚ〕adv. ~也不（接於否定子句之後）

anyone else 任何其他的人

30. (**C**)　M：Can you give me a discount on this bag?

W：Well, I guess I can give you ten percent off.

M：How about fifteen?

W：No.　That's my final offer.

M：Okay.　Here's 900 dollars.

Question：How much money did the woman get for
the bag?

A. Ten percent.

B. 1000 dollars.

C. 900 dollars.

* give〔gɪv〕v. 給　　discount〔'dɪskaʊnt〕n. 折扣

bag〔bæg〕n. 袋子

well〔wɛl〕interj. 好吧（表讓步）

guess〔gɛs〕v. 猜想；認為

percent〔pə'sɛnt〕n. 百分之…

ten percent off 打九折　　***How about~?*** ～如何？

final〔'faɪnḷ〕adj. 最後的

offer〔'ɔfə〕n. 報價；開價

okay〔'o'ke〕adv. 好（＝ *OK*）

Here is~. 這是～。　　get〔gɛt〕v. 得到

全民英語能力分級檢定測驗
初級測驗⑩

　　本測驗分三部份，全爲三選一之選擇題，每部份各 10 題，共 30 題，作答時間約 20 分鐘。

第一部份：看圖辨義

　　　　　本部份共 10 題，試題冊上每題有一個圖片，請聽錄音機播出一個相關的問題，與 A、B、C 三個英語敘述後，選一個與所看到圖片最相符的答案，並在答案紙上相對的圓圈內塗黑作答。每題播出一遍，問題及選項均不印在試題冊上。

例：（看）

（聽）

Look at the picture.　How much is the hamburger?

　　A.　It's eighty dollars.
　　B.　It's fifty-five dollars.
　　C.　It's eighteen dollars.

正確答案爲 A

Questions 1

Question 2

Question 3

Questions 4

Question 5

請 翻 頁

Question 6

Question 7

Question 8

Question 9

Question 10

請翻頁 ▯▯⟹

第二部份： 問答

本部份共 10 題，每題錄音機會播出一個問句或直述句，每題播出一次，聽後請從試題冊上 A、B、C 三個選項中，選出一個最適合的回答或回應，並在答案紙上塗黑作答。

例：

（聽） Good morning, Kevin. How are you?

（看） A. I'm fine, thank you.
　　　 B. I'm in the living room.
　　　 C. My name is Kevin.

正確答案為 A

11. A. Yes. I usually watch it on TV.
　　B. I swim, play basketball and jog.
　　C. Sure. But we need some more people.

12. A. She was born in May.
　　B. It's always in May.
　　C. She's at a meeting today.

13. A. Since I was five.
    B. From two to four
       every day.
    C. Whenever I can.

14. A. It's over there on
       your left.
    B. When is it?
    C. I'm not sure.

15. A. Yes, thank you.
    B. Next to the window.
    C. I'm sorry, but that
       seat is taken.

16. A. Japan.
    B. September.
    C. I did.

17. A. I won't.
    B. I have.
    C. I should.

18. A. Turn around very
       slowly.
    B. You can give it to me.
    C. Take a left at the next
       corner.

19. A. What's wrong with her?
    B. She certainly is!
    C. But I like her.

20. A. No, I can't.
    B. It's on the second shelf.
    C. Because we don't
       have any.

請 翻 頁 ‖⟹

第三部份： 簡短對話

　　本部份共 10 題，每題錄音機會播出一段對話及一個相關的問題，每題播出兩次，聽後請從試題冊上 A、B、C 三個選項中，選出一個最適合的回答，並在答案紙上塗黑作答。

例：

（聽）(Woman)　Good afternoon, …Mr. Davis?

　　　(Man)　　　Yes.　I have an appointment with Dr. Sanders at two o'clock.　My son Tommy has a fever.

　　　(Woman)　Oh, that's too bad.　Well, please have a seat, Mr. Davis.　Dr. Sanders will be right with you.

　　　Question:　Where did this conversation take place?

（看）A.　In a post office.

　　　B.　In a restaurant.

　　　C.　In a doctor's office.

　　　正確答案爲 C

21. A. It is near the first bus
      stop.

    B. It is near the park.

    C. It is after the bus
      station.

22. A. She thinks they will
      not be so terrible then.

    B. The store will have a
      new style of curtains
      for sale then.

    C. They will be cheaper
      then.

23. A. She was watching a
      movie.

    B. She was smoking in
      the wrong place.

    C. She went outside the
      theater.

24. A. They will pay it
      together.

    B. They will go to a
      bank.

    C. They will use their
      credit cards.

25. A. Yes, even though
      they are expensive.

    B. Yes, if they are
      cheaper at the other
      market.

    C. No. There are not
      any mangoes in the
      market.

請 翻 頁 ⟹

26. A. She forgot to take
　　　 them out of the door.
　　 B. They are missing.
　　 C. She gave them to
　　　 the man.

27. A. At eight o'clock.
　　 B. About ten to eight.
　　 C. Around a quarter
　　　 after eight.

28. A. The woman will do it.
　　 B. The man will.
　　 C. He will get some
　　　 more.

29. A. She caught the flu.
　　 B. She ate some bad
　　　 food.
　　 C. She needs a
　　　 vacation.

30. A. He fell behind in
　　　 his work.
　　 B. He didn't give her
　　　 the report on time.
　　 C. He gave her the
　　　 report yesterday.

初級英語聽力檢定⑩詳解

第一部份

Look at the picture for question 1.

1. (**B**) How is the egg cooked?

    A. Yes, it is.　　　　B. It is fried.

    C. It is delicious.

    * egg〔εg〕*n.* 蛋　　cook〔kʊk〕*v.* 煮
    fry〔fraɪ〕*v.* 煎　　delicious〔dɪ'lɪʃəs〕*adj.* 美味的

Look at the picture for question 2.

2. (**B**) Why is the man pointing?

    A. It is a clock.　　　B. The worker is late.

    C. He is sad.

    * point〔pɔɪnt〕*v.* 指著　　clock〔klɑk〕*n.* 時鐘
    worker〔'wɝkɚ〕*n.* 工人　　late〔let〕*adj.* 遲到的
    sad〔sæd〕*adj.* 傷心的

Look at the picture for question 3.

3. (**A**) Who will be in the photo?

    A. A couple.　　　　B. A photographer.

    C. There are two.

    * photo〔'foto〕*n.* 照片 (= *photograph*)
    couple〔'kʌpl̩〕*n.* 一對男女；夫妻
    photographer〔fə'tɑgrəfɚ〕*n.* 攝影師

Look at the picture for question 4.

4. (**C**) What is wrong?

    A. Her finger.

    B. The woman did it.

    C. She cut herself.

    * ***What is wrong?*** 怎麼了？

        finger〔'fɪŋgɚ〕*n.* 手指　　cut〔kʌt〕*v.* 切

        herself〔hɚ'sɛlf〕*pron.* 她自己

Look at the picture for question 5.

5. (**C**) Where is the bathtub?

    A. Yes, he is.

    B. A boy.

    C. The bathroom.

    * bathtub〔'bæθ,tʌb〕*n.* 浴缸

      bathroom〔'bæθ,rum〕*n.* 浴室

Look at the picture for question 6.

6. (**B**) What is the woman on the right doing?

    A. She is in the hospital.

    B. She is visiting.

    C. She brought flowers.

    * right〔raɪt〕*n.* 右邊　　hospital〔'hɑspɪtḷ〕*n.* 醫院

      visit〔'vɪzɪt〕*v.* 探望；參觀　　bring〔brɪŋ〕*v.* 帶來

      flower〔'flauɚ〕*n.* 花

Look at the picture for question 7.

7. (**A**) What is on the hat?
    A. Stars.   B. The clown's head.
    C. It is a clown hat.

    * hat〔hæt〕*n.* 帽子   star〔stɑr〕*n.* 星星
    clown〔klaʊn〕*n.* 小丑   head〔hɛd〕*n.* 頭

Look at the picture for question 8.

8. (**C**) Who is giving money?
    A. The beggar did.   B. He is poor.
    C. A boy.

    * beggar〔'bɛgɚ〕*n.* 乞丐   poor〔pʊr〕*adj.* 窮的

Look at the picture for question 9.

9. (**B**) What is the woman pointing at?
    A. You can't smoke here.
    B. A no-smoking sign.
    C. Because the man is smoking.

    * point〔pɔɪnt〕*v.* 指著   smoke〔smok〕*v.* 抽煙
    no-smoking〔ˌno'smokɪŋ〕*adj.* 禁止吸煙的
    sign〔saɪn〕*n.* 告示；標誌

Look at the picture for question 10.

10. (**B**) Where is the candle?
    A. There is one candle.   B. On the table.
    C. It is her birthday.

    * candle〔'kændḷ〕*n.* 蠟燭   table〔'tebḷ〕*n.* 桌子

第二部份

11. (**B**) Do you play any sports?

    A. Yes. I usually watch it on TV.

    B. I swim, play basketball and jog.

    C. Sure. But we need some more people.

    * play〔ple〕v. 做（運動）   sport〔sport〕n. 運動
      usually〔'juʒʊəlɪ〕adv. 通常   swim〔swɪm〕v. 游泳
      basketball〔'bæskɪt,bɔl〕n. 籃球
      jog〔dʒɑg〕v. 慢跑   sure〔ʃʊr〕adv. 好；沒問題
      need〔nid〕v. 需要   more〔mor〕adj. 更多的

12. (**B**) When is Mother's Day?

    A. She was born in May.

    B. It's always in May.

    C. She's at a meeting today.

    * *Mother's Day* 母親節   born〔bɔrn〕adj. 出生的
      May〔me〕n. 五月   always〔'ɔlwez〕adv. 總是
      meeting〔'mitɪŋ〕n. 會議

13. (**A**) How long have you been playing the piano?

    A. Since I was five.

    B. From two to four every day.

    C. Whenever I can.

    * *How long ~?* ～多久？   play〔ple〕v. 演奏
      piano〔pɪ'æno〕n. 鋼琴   *play the piano* 彈鋼琴
      since〔sɪns〕conj. 自從
      whenever〔hwɛn'ɛvɚ〕conj. 無論何時（只要）

14. (**C**) Did you pass the chemistry test?

    A. It's over there on your left.

    B. When is it?

    C. I'm not sure.

    * pass〔pæs〕*v.* 通過（考試）

      chemistry〔'kɛmɪstrɪ〕*n.* 化學

      test〔tɛst〕*n.* 考試   ***over there*** 在那裡

      left〔lɛft〕*n.* 左邊   sure〔ʃʊr〕*adj.* 確定的

15. (**B**) Where would you like to sit?

    A. Yes, thank you.

    B. Next to the window.

    C. I'm sorry, but that seat is taken.

    * ***would like*** 想要（＝*want*）   sit〔sɪt〕*v.* 坐

      next to … 在…旁邊   seat〔sit〕*n.* 座位

      take〔tek〕*v.* 佔（位子）

      That seat is taken. 那個位子有人坐了。

16. (**B**) When did you take your vacation last year?

    A. Japan.   B. September.   C. I did.

    * vacation〔ve'keʃən〕*n.* 假期   ***take a vacation*** 度假

      Japan〔dʒə'pæn〕*n.* 日本

      September〔sɛp'tɛmbə〕*n.* 九月

17. (**A**) Don't forget to bring a jacket.

    A. I won't.   B. I have.   C. I should.

    * forget〔fə'gɛt〕*v.* 忘記   bring〔brɪŋ〕*v.* 帶

      jacket〔'dʒækɪt〕*n.* 夾克   should〔ʃʊd〕*aux.* 應該

18. (**C**)　Where should I turn?
　　　　A. Turn around very slowly.
　　　　B. You can give it to me.
　　　　C. Take a left at the next corner.

　　　　* turn〔tɝn〕*v.* 轉向　　***turn around*** 轉過身去
　　　　　slowly〔'sloli〕*adv.* 慢慢地
　　　　　give sth. to sb. 給某人某物　　***take a left*** 向左轉
　　　　　next〔nɛkst〕*adj.* 下一個　　corner〔'kɔrnɚ〕*n.* 轉角

19. (**A**)　Did you see Marge this morning?　She looks terrible!
　　　　A. What's wrong with her?
　　　　B. She certainly is!　　C. But I like her.

　　　　* look〔luk〕*v.* 看起來　　terrible〔'tɛrəbl̩〕*adj.* 很糟的
　　　　　What's wrong with ～? ～怎麼了；～哪裡不對勁？
　　　　　certainly〔'sɝtn̩lɪ〕*adv.* 必定　　like〔laɪk〕*v.* 喜歡

20. (**B**)　Where can I find the soap?
　　　　A. No, I can't.　　　　B. It's on the second shelf.
　　　　C. Because we don't have any.

　　　　* find〔faɪnd〕*v.* 找到　　soap〔sop〕*n.* 肥皂
　　　　　second〔'sɛkənd〕*adj.* 第二的　　shelf〔ʃɛlf〕*n.* 架子
　　　　　because〔bɪ'kɔz〕*conj.* 因為　　any〔'ɛnɪ〕*pron.* 任何人或物

第三部份

21. (**B**)　M：I want to go to the post office.　Is this the right bus?
　　　　W：Yes.　It will go past the post office.
　　　　M：Do you know the name of the stop?
　　　　W：No, but get off at the first stop after the park.
　　　　M：Thanks.

Question：Where is the post office?

A. It is near the first bus stop.

B. It is near the park.

C. It is after the bus station.

* **post office** 郵局　　right〔raɪt〕adj. 正確的
　past〔pæst〕prep. 經過　　stop〔stɑp〕n. 停車站
　get off 下車　　near〔nɪr〕prep. 在…附近
　bus stop 公車站　　after〔'æftɚ〕prep. 在…之後
　bus station 公車總站

22. (**C**)　M：Let's get some new curtains. These look terrible.

W：I'd rather wait until next month.

M：Why?

W：The department store is going to have a sale then.

Question：Why does the woman want to buy curtains
　　　　　next month?

A. She thinks they will not be so terrible then.

B. The store will have a new style of curtains for sale
　then.

C. They will be cheaper then.

* get〔gɛt〕v. 買　　curtain〔'kɝtn〕n. 窗簾
　look〔lʊk〕v. 看起來　　terrible〔'tɛrəbl〕adj. 很糟的
　would rather V. 寧願～　　wait〔wet〕v. 等待
　until〔ən'tɪl〕prep. 直到　　month〔mʌnθ〕n. 月
　department store 百貨公司　　sale〔sel〕n. 拍賣
　then〔ðɛn〕adv. 到那時　　think〔θɪŋk〕v. 認為
　style〔staɪl〕n. 樣式　　**for sale** 出售
　cheaper〔'tʃipɚ〕adj. 較便宜的（cheap 的比較級）

23. (**B**) M：Excuse me. There is no smoking allowed in the
theater.

W：Oh, sorry. Where can I go?

M：You can finish your cigarette outside.

Question：What was the woman doing wrong?

A. She was watching a movie.

B. She was smoking in the wrong place.

C. She went outside the theater.

* ***Excuse me.*** 不好意思；對不起。
   smoke〔smok〕*v.* 抽煙   allow〔ə'lau〕*v.* 允許
   no smoking allowed 禁止吸煙   theater〔'θiətə〕*n.* 戲院
   oh〔o〕*interj.* 喔（因驚訝所發出的感嘆）
   finish〔'fɪnɪʃ〕*v.* 完成；做完（在此指「抽完」）
   cigarette〔͵sɪgə'rɛt, 'sɪgə͵rɛt〕*n.* 香煙
   outside〔'aut'said〕*adv.* 在外面
   wrong〔rɔŋ〕*adv.* 錯誤地   *adj.* 錯誤的；不對的
   place〔ples〕*n.* 地方；場所
   watch〔watʃ〕*v.* 看（電影、電視）
   movie〔'muvɪ〕*n.* 電影

24. (**A**) M：Oh, no! I don't have enough money to pay the bill.

W：Don't worry. I have a credit card.

M：So do I, but they take only cash here.

W：Then let's pay the bill together. I'm sure we have
enough money between us.

Question：How will they pay the bill?

A. They will pay it together.
B. They will go to a bank.
C. They will use their credit cards.

* ***Oh, no!*** 噢，糟了！　　enough〔ə'nʌf〕*adj.* 足夠的
pay〔pe〕*v.* 支付　　bill〔bɪl〕*n.* 帳單
worry〔'wɜɪ〕*v.* 擔心　　credit〔'krɛdɪt〕*n.* 信用
credit card 信用卡
So do I. 我也是。（在這裡作「我也有。」解）
take〔tek〕*v.* 接受　　only〔'onlɪ〕*adv.* 只
cash〔kæʃ〕*n.* 現金　　then〔ðɛn〕*adv.* 那麼
together〔tə'gɛðɚ〕*adv.* 一起　　sure〔ʃʊr〕*adj.* 確信的
between〔bə'twin〕*prep.* 在…之間（表共有）
we have enough money between us 我們的錢加起來足夠了
bank〔bæŋk〕*n.* 銀行　　use〔juz〕*v.* 使用

25.(**B**)　M：Do you like mangoes?
　　　　　W：Yes, very much.　Why don't we buy some?
　　　　　M：Okay, but these are too expensive.　Let's look for
　　　　　　　some at the other market.
　　　　　Question：Will they buy mangoes?
　　　　　A. Yes, even though they are expensive.
　　　　　B. Yes, if they are cheaper at the other market.
　　　　　C. No.　There are not any mangoes in the market.

* mango〔'mæŋgo〕*n.* 芒果
Why don't we ~? 我們為何不 ~ ？（表提議）
buy〔baɪ〕*v.* 買　　okay〔'o'ke〕*adv.* 好（= *OK*）
expensive〔ɪk'spɛnsɪv〕*adj.* 昂貴的
look for 尋找　　***the other***（兩者中）另一個
market〔'mɑrkɪt〕*n.* 市場　　***even though*** 即使

26. (**A**)　M：Are these your keys?

W：Yes, they are.　Where did you find them?

M：They were still in the door.

W：Oh, how careless of me.

Question：What happened to the woman's keys?

A.　She forgot to take them out of the door.

B.　They are missing.

C.　She gave them to the man.

* key〔ki〕*n.* 鑰匙　　find〔faɪnd〕*v.* 找到

still〔stɪl〕*adv.* 仍然

oh〔o〕*interj.* 喔（因驚訝所發出的感嘆）

careless〔'kɛrlɪs〕*adj.* 粗心的；不小心的

How careless of me! 我真粗心；我真不小心！

happen〔'hæpən〕*v.* 發生

forget〔fə'gɛt〕*v.* 忘記

take…out of ～ 把…從～拿出來

missing〔'mɪsɪŋ〕*adj.* 失蹤的；找不到的

27. (**C**)　M：What time does the party start?

W：The invitation says eight o'clock, but I'd like to arrive a few minutes after that.

M：OK.　Let's leave here about ten to eight.

Question：When will they arrive at the party?

A. At eight o'clock.

B. About ten to eight.

C. Around a quarter after eight.

* ***what time*** 幾點　　start〔stɑrt〕*v.* 開始

invitation〔͵ɪnvə'teʃən〕*n.* 邀請函

say〔se〕*v.* 寫著　　***would like to V.*** 想要～（= *want to V.*）

arrive〔ə'raɪv〕*v.* 抵達　　***a few*** 一些

minute〔'mɪnɪt〕*n.* 分鐘　　after〔'æftɚ〕*prep.* 在…之後

leave〔liv〕*v.* 離開

ten to eight 七點五十分；再過十分鐘就八點

around〔ə'raʊnd〕*adv.* 大約

quarter〔'kwɔrtɚ〕*n.* 一刻鐘；十五分鐘

28. (**B**) M：Is there any more milk?

W：No. That's all there is.

M：Well, I'm going to finish it.

W：That's all right. I'll get some more today.

Question：Who will drink the milk?

A. The woman will do it.

B. The man will.

C. He will get some more.

* any〔'ɛnɪ〕*adj.* 絲毫的　　more〔mor〕*adj.* 多餘的

milk〔mɪlk〕*n.* 牛奶

That's all there is. 全部就這麼多了。

well〔wɛl〕*interj.* 那麼（用於繼續話題時）

finish〔'fɪnɪʃ〕*v.* 完成；做完（在此指「喝完」）

That's all right. 沒關係。　　get〔gɛt〕*v.* 買

get some more 再多買一些　　drink〔drɪŋk〕*v.* 喝

29. (**A**)　M：You don't look so good.　What happened?

　　　　　W：I got sick while on vacation.

　　　　　M：Was it bad food?

　　　　　W：No.　The flu.

　　　　　Question：Why does the woman look sick?

　　　　　A. She caught the flu.

　　　　　B. She ate some bad food.

　　　　　C. She needs a vacation.

　　　*　***You don't look so good.*** 你看起來不太好。

　　　　What happened? 發生了什麼事？

　　　　get sick 生病　　while〔hwaɪl〕*conj.* 當…的時候

　　　　on vacation 休假中　　***Was it bad food?*** 是吃壞肚子嗎？

　　　　flu〔flu〕*n.* 流行性感冒　　***look sick*** 臉色不好

　　　　catch〔kætʃ〕*v.* 染上（病）（三態變化為：catch-caught-caught）

　　　　need〔nid〕*v.* 需要　　vacation〔ve'keʃən〕*n.* 假期

30. (**B**)　M：Here is that report you wanted.

　　　　　W：Thanks, but I wanted it yesterday.

　　　　　M：Sorry.　I'm really behind in my work.

　　　　　Question：What didn't the man do?

　　　　　A. He fell behind in his work.

　　　　　B. He didn't give her the report on time.

　　　　　C. He gave her the report yesterday.

　　　*　***Here is～.*** 這是～。　　report〔rɪ'port〕*n.* 報告

　　　　want〔want〕*v.* 想要　　really〔'riəlɪ〕*adv.* 的確

　　　　behind〔bɪ'haɪnd〕*adv.* 落後

　　　　fall behind 落後　　***on time*** 準時

全民英語能力分級檢定測驗
初級測驗⑪

本測驗分三部份，全為三選一之選擇題，每部份各 10 題，共 30 題，作答時間約 20 分鐘。

第一部份：看圖辨義

本部份共 10 題，試題冊上每題有一個圖片，請聽錄音機播出一個相關的問題，與 A、B、C 三個英語敘述後，選一個與所看到圖片最相符的答案，並在答案紙上相對的圓圈內塗黑作答。每題播出一遍，問題及選項均不印在試題冊上。

例：（看）

NT$80　　NT$50

（聽）

Look at the picture.　How much is the hamburger?

A. It's eighty dollars.
B. It's fifty-five dollars.
C. It's eighteen dollars.

正確答案為 A

Questions 1

Question 2

Questions 3

Question 4

請翻頁

Question 5

Question 6

Question 7

Question 8

Question 9

Question 10

請 翻 頁 ▯⟹

第二部份：問答

本部份共 10 題，每題錄音機會播出一個問句或直述句，每題播出一次，聽後請從試題冊上 A、B、C 三個選項中，選出一個最適合的回答或回應，並在答案紙上塗黑作答。

例：

（聽）　Good morning, Kevin.　How are you?

（看）　A.　I'm fine, thank you.
　　　　 B.　I'm in the living room.
　　　　 C.　My name is Kevin.

正確答案爲 A

11. A. It cost 50 dollars.
　　 B. Around the corner.
　　 C. Five minutes ago.

12. A. No, thanks. I can't drink milk.
　　 B. Yes, it looks like melon.
　　 C. Yes, I would. It looks delicious.

13. A. Ham and cheese, please.
　　 B. It's a tuna sandwich.
　　 C. I'll have it on the table.

14. A. Pets aren't allowed in this building.
　　 B. At the pet shop.
　　 C. Because it ran away.

15. A. Where will he stay?

    B. How will it get home?

    C. I think I'll stay home
    then.

16. A. Oh, it was nothing.

    B. Okay. There he is!

    C. Don't worry. We'll
    win next time.

17. A. Thirteen.

    B. On the thirtieth of May.

    C. In Taichung.

18. A. There is a convenience
    store across the street.

    B. Yes, but it's a little
    expensive here.

    C. Yes, thanks. I'll have
    a Coke.

19. A. No. I don't like
    children.

    B. My older sister
    often took care of
    me.

    C. I began babysitting
    when I was fifteen.

20. A. Yes, I know him
    very well.

    B. Pleased to meet
    you, Frank.

    C. We were classmates
    in elementary
    school.

請 翻 頁 ⇒

第三部份： 簡短對話

本部份共 10 題，每題錄音機會播出一段對話及一個相關的問題，每題播出兩次，聽後請從試題冊上 A、B、C 三個選項中，選出一個最適合的回答，並在答案紙上塗黑作答。

例：

(聽)(Woman) Good afternoon, …Mr. Davis?

(Man) Yes. I have an appointment with Dr. Sanders at two o'clock. My son Tommy has a fever.

(Woman) Oh, that's too bad. Well, please have a seat, Mr. Davis. Dr. Sanders will be right with you.

Question: Where did this conversation take place?

(看) A. In a post office.
B. In a restaurant.
C. In a doctor's office.

正確答案爲 C

21. A. He can go every
     Monday.
   B. He can go at 9:00 today.
   C. He can go now.

22. A. The dentist will fix the
     woman's tooth.
   B. The woman will see a
     different dentist
     tomorrow.
   C. The dentist will put a
     hole in her tooth.

23. A. He ordered a cold meal.
   B. He will have a beer
     with his dinner.
   C. Yes, he is old enough
     to drink beer.

24. A. To Singapore.
   B. The man did.
   C. No, she didn't.

25. A. The man did.
   B. A doctor.
   C. A salesperson.

26. A. They will play a
     game.
   B. They will play
     some music.
   C. They will play in
     the water.

請 翻 頁 ⟹

27. A. They are 400 dollars.
    B. They are for the 7:30 show.
    C. They are for three people.

28. A. At least five days a week.
    B. Every ten minutes.
    C. As long as it is possible.

29. A. She does not like to touch animals.
    B. She broke her neck.
    C. She is afraid that she will get hurt.

30. A. Buy the coat even if he doesn't like it.
    B. Buy a brown coat.
    C. Buy the cheapest coat.

初級英語聽力檢定⑪詳解

第一部份

Look at the picture for question 1.

1. (**A**) What is the woman doing?
    A. She is cleaning.
    B. She is angry.
    C. She wants him to help her.

    * clean〔klin〕*v.* 打掃   angry〔'æŋgrɪ〕*adj.* 生氣的
    want sb. to V. 想要某人～   help〔hɛlp〕*v.* 幫助

Look at the picture for question 2.

2. (**B**) How is she eating it?
    A. It is candy.
    B. She is licking it.
    C. She likes it very much.

    * candy〔'kændɪ〕*n.* 糖果
    lick〔lɪk〕*v.* 舔   like〔laɪk〕*v.* 喜歡

Look at the picture for question 3.

3. (**C**) What is the girl flying?
    A. No, she is on the ground.
    B. In the air.   C. A kite.

    * fly〔flaɪ〕*v.* 放（風箏）（三態變化為：fly-flew-flown）
    ground〔graʊnd〕*n.* 地面   ***in the air*** 在空中
    kite〔kaɪt〕*n.* 風箏

Look at the picture for question 4.

4. (**B**)　Where are they?

　　A. Doctors.

　　B. A hospital.

　　C. They can operate.

　　* doctor〔'dɑktɚ〕*n.* 醫生

　　　hospital〔'hɑspɪtḷ〕*n.* 醫院

　　　operate〔'ɑpə,ret〕*v.* 開刀；動手術

Look at the picture for question 5.

5. (**A**)　What is she holding?

　　A. A comb.

　　B. A mirror.

　　C. Her hair.

　　* hold〔hold〕*v.* 拿著；握著　　comb〔kom〕*n.* 梳子

　　　mirror〔'mɪrɚ〕*n.* 鏡子　　hair〔hɛr〕*n.* 頭髮

Look at the picture for question 6.

6. (**C**)　Who brought it?

　　A. A letter.

　　B. In the mailbox.

　　C. A mailman.

　　* bring〔brɪŋ〕*v.* 帶來（三態變化為：bring-brought-brought）

　　　letter〔'lɛtɚ〕*n.* 信　　mailbox〔'mel,bɑks〕*n.* 郵筒

　　　mailman〔'mel,mæn〕*n.* 郵差

Look at the picture for question 7.

7. (**A**) How does he feel?

    A. He is tired.

    B. He is shouting.

    C. He is sleeping.

    * feel〔fil〕*v.* 感覺　　tired〔taɪrd〕*adj.* 疲倦的

      shout〔ʃaʊt〕*v.* 大叫　　sleep〔slip〕*v.* 睡覺

Look at the picture for question 8.

8. (**B**) Why is he taking medicine?

    A. He is in bed.

    B. He is sick.

    C. It tastes terrible.

    * ***take medicine*** 吃藥　　***be in bed*** 躺在床上

      sick〔sɪk〕*adj.* 生病的　　taste〔test〕*v.* 嚐起來

      terrible〔'tɛləbļ〕*adj.* 可怕的；噁心的

Look at the picture for question 9.

9. (**C**) Where can you buy these?

    A. A pencil, eraser and notebook.

    B. Yes, they are not expensive.

    C. In a stationery store.

    * eraser〔ɪ'resɚ〕*n.* 橡皮擦

      notebook〔'not،bʊk〕*n.* 筆記本

      expensive〔ɪk'spɛnsɪv〕*adj.* 昂貴的

      stationery〔'steʃən،ɛrɪ〕*n.* 文具

      stationery store 文具行

Look at the picture for question 10.

10. (**C**) What is the waiter doing?

    A. They are waiting for their dinner.

    B. He will wait for them.

    C. He is serving food.

    * waiter (ˈwetɚ) *n.* 服務生　***wait for*** 等待
      serve (sɜv) *v.* 供應；端出　food (fud) *n.* 食物

第二部份

11. (**B**) Where did you park your car?

    A. It cost 50 dollars.

    B. Around the corner.

    C. Five minutes ago.

    * park (pɑrk) *v.* 停 (車)
      cost (kɔst) *v.* 值…(錢)　dollar (ˈdɑlɚ) *n.* 元
      around (əˈraʊnd) *prep.* 在…附近
      corner (ˈkɔrnɚ) *n.* 轉角　minute (ˈmɪnɪt) *n.* 分鐘
      ago (əˈgo) *adv.* …以前

12. (**C**) Would you like some melon?

    A. No, thanks. I can't drink milk.

    B. Yes, it looks like melon.

    C. Yes, I would. It looks delicious.

    * ***would like*** 想要 (= *want*)　melon (ˈmɛlən) *n.* 甜瓜
      drink (drɪŋk) *v.* 喝　milk (mɪlk) *n.* 牛奶
      look like 看起像　delicious (dɪˈlɪʃəs) *adj.* 美味的

13. (**A**) What do you want on your sandwich?

  A. Ham and cheese, please.

  B. It's a tuna sandwich.

  C. I'll have it on the table.

  * sandwich〔'sændwɪtʃ〕 *n.* 三明治

  What do you want on your sandwich? 你想要加什麼
  在你的三明治裡？

  ham〔hæm〕 *n.* 火腿 cheese〔tʃiz〕 *n.* 起司

  tuna〔'tunə〕 *n.* 鮪魚 have〔hæv〕 *v.* 吃

14. (**A**) Why don't we get a dog?

  A. Pets aren't allowed in this building.

  B. At the pet shop.

  C. Because it ran away.

  * get〔gɛt〕 *v.* 買 pet〔pɛt〕 *n.* 寵物

  allow〔ə'laʊ〕 *v.* 允許

  building〔'bɪldɪŋ〕 *n.* 建築物；大樓

  shop〔ʃɑp〕 *n.* 商店 because〔bɪ'kɔz〕 *conj.* 因為

  run away 逃跑

15. (**C**) A big storm is coming tomorrow.

  A. Where will he stay?

  B. How will it get home?

  C. I think I'll stay home then.

  * storm〔stɔrm〕 *n.* 暴風雨 stay〔ste〕 *v.* 停留

  get〔gɛt〕 *v.* 抵達 then〔ðɛn〕 *adv.* 到那時

16. (**B**) Let's congratulate Ted on winning the game.

   A. Oh, it was nothing.

   B. Okay. There he is!

   C. Don't worry. We'll win next time.

   * congratulate〔kən'grætʃə,let〕v. 恭喜
     congratulate sb. on ~ 恭喜某人～
     win〔wɪn〕v. 贏得　　game〔gem〕n. 比賽
     It was nothing. 那沒什麼。
     okay〔'o'ke〕adv. 好（= OK）　　***There he is!*** 他來了！
     worry〔'wɝɪ〕v. 擔心　　***next time*** 下一次

17. (**B**) When were you born?

   A. Thirteen.

   B. On the thirtieth of May.

   C. In Taichung.

   * born〔bɔrn〕adj. 出生的　　thirteen〔θɝ'tin〕n. 十三歲
     thirtieth〔'θɝtɪɪθ〕n.（每月的）三十日
     May〔me〕n. 五月　　Taichung〔'taɪ'tʃuŋ〕n. 台中

18. (**A**) Where can I buy something to drink?

   A. There is a convenience store across the street.

   B. Yes, but it's a little expensive here.

   C. Yes, thanks. I'll have a Coke.

   * drink〔drɪŋk〕v. 喝　　***convenience store*** 便利商店
     across〔ə'krɔs〕prep. 在…對面　　street〔strit〕n. 街道
     a little 有一點　　expensive〔ɪk'spɛnsɪv〕adj. 昂貴的
     have〔hæv〕v. 吃；喝　　Coke〔kok〕n. 可口可樂

19. (**B**) Did you have a babysitter when you were younger?

    A. No. I don't like children.

    B. My older sister often took care of me.

    C. I began babysitting when I was fifteen.

* babysitter〔'bebɪ,sɪtɚ 〕*n.* 臨時保姆（= *baby-sitter* ）
  younger〔'jʌŋgɚ 〕*adj.* 較年輕的（young 的比較級）
  children〔'tʃɪldrən 〕*n. pl.* 小孩（child 的複數）
  older sister 姊姊（= *elder sister* ）
  often〔'ɔfən 〕*adv.* 經常   ***take care of*** 照顧
  begin〔bɪ'gɪn 〕*v.* 開始（三態變化為：begin-began-begun ）
  babysit〔'bebɪ,sɪt 〕*v.* 當臨時保姆（= *baby-sit* ）
  fifteen〔fɪf'tin 〕*n.* 十五歲

20. (**A**) How do you know Frank?

    A. Yes, I know him very well.

    B. Pleased to meet you, Frank.

    C. We were classmates in elementary school.

* ***How do you know~?*** 你有多了解～？
  well〔wɛl 〕*adv.* 充分地；全然地
  Pleased to meet you. 很高興認識你。
  classmate〔'klæs,met 〕*n.* 同班同學
  elementary〔,ɛlə'mɛntərɪ 〕*adj.* 初等的
  elementary school 小學

第三部份

21. (**B**) M：Is the library open today?

　　　　W：Yes. It's open every day except Mondays.

　　　　M：Then I'll go now.

　　　　W：But it doesn't open until 9:00.

　　　　Question：When can the man go to the library?

　　　A. He can go every Monday.

　　　B. He can go at 9:00 today.

　　　C. He can go now.

　　　* library〔'laɪˌbrɛrɪ〕*n.* 圖書館

　　　　open〔'opɛn〕*adj.* 開著的 *v.* 開門

　　　　except〔ɪk'sɛpt〕*prep.* 除了…以外

　　　　then〔ðɛn〕*adv.* 那麼　　***not…until~*** 直到～才…

22. (**A**) M：How was your trip to the dentist?

　　　　W：Terrible! I have a hole in my tooth.

　　　　M：Did he fix it?

　　　　W：No. I have to go back tomorrow.

　　　　Question：What will happen tomorrow?

　　　A. The dentist will fix the woman's tooth.

　　　B. The woman will see a different dentist tomorrow.

　　　C. The dentist will put a hole in her tooth.

　　　* trip〔trɪp〕*n.* 外出；走一趟　　dentist〔'dɛntɪst〕*n.* 牙醫

　　　　terrible〔'tɛrəbḷ〕*adj.* 可怕的　　hole〔hol〕*n.* 洞

　　　　tooth〔tuθ〕*n.* 牙齒（複數形爲 teeth〔tiθ〕）

　　　　fix〔fɪks〕*v.* 修補　　happen〔'hæpən〕*v.* 發生

　　　　different〔'dɪfərənt〕*adj.* 不一樣的　　put〔pʊt〕*v.* 放

23. (**B**)　M：Please bring me the fish and a small salad.

　　　　　W：Anything to drink?

　　　　　M：Yes. I'll have a beer, but make sure it's a cold one.

　　　　　W：Of course, sir.

　　　　Question：What did the man order?

　　　　A. He ordered a cold meal.

　　　　B. He will have a beer with his dinner.

　　　　C. Yes, he is old enough to drink beer.

　　　＊ bring〔brɪŋ〕*v.* 帶（東西）來（給人）

　　　　fish〔fɪʃ〕*n.* 魚　　salad〔'sæləd〕*n.* 沙拉

　　　　Anything to drink? 要喝什麼嗎？

　　　　have〔hæv〕*v.* 吃；喝　　beer〔bɪr〕*n.* 啤酒

　　　　make sure 確定　　cold〔kold〕*adj.* 冷的；冰過的

　　　　of course 當然　　sir〔sɝ〕*n.* 先生

　　　　order〔'ɔrdɚ〕*v.* 點（菜）　　meal〔mil〕*n.* 一餐

　　　　dinner〔'dɪnɚ〕*n.* 晚餐　　enough〔ə'nʌf〕*adv.* 足夠地

24. (**B**)　M：Where did you spend the winter vacation?

　　　　　W：I stayed here. How about you?

　　　　　M：I went to Singapore with my family.

　　　　Question：Who traveled during the winter vacation?

　　　　A. To Singapore.　　B. The man did.

　　　　C. No, she didn't.

　　　＊ spend〔spɛnd〕*v.* 度過　　***winter vacation*** 寒假

　　　　stay〔ste〕*v.* 停留　　***How about you?*** 你呢？

　　　　Singapore〔'sɪŋgə,por〕*n.* 新加坡

　　　　travel〔'trævl̩〕*v.* 旅行　　during〔'djʊrɪŋ〕*prep.* 在…期間

25. (**C**)   M: Did I hear the phone ring?

W: Yes. It was just a sales call.

M: What for?

W: That new health club.

Question: Who called?

A. The man did.

B. A doctor.

C. A salesperson.

* hear〔hɪr〕*v.* 聽到
   phone〔fon〕*n.* 電話 (= *telephone*)
   ring〔rɪŋ〕*v.* (鈴) 響   just〔dʒʌst〕*adv.* 只是
   sales〔selz〕*adj.* 銷售的   ***sales call*** 推銷電話
   What for? 有什麼目的？   health〔hɛlθ〕*n.* 健康
   club〔klʌb〕*n.* 俱樂部   call〔kɔl〕*v.* 打電話
   doctor〔'dɑktɚ〕*n.* 醫生
   salesperson〔'selz͵pɝsn̩〕*n.* 業務員；推銷員

26. (**A**)   M: Let's go to the beach.

W: No. It's too cold to swim and I don't want to just
   sit there.

M: I'll bring the Frisbee and we can play.

W: Okay.

Question: What will they do?

A.　They will play a game.

B.　They will play some music.

C.　They will play in the water.

* beach〔bitʃ〕*n.* 海邊　　***too…to～*** 太…以致不能～
cold〔kold〕*adj.* 寒冷的　　swim〔swɪm〕*v.* 游泳
just〔dʒʌst〕*adv.* 只是　　sit〔sɪt〕*v.* 坐
bring〔brɪŋ〕*v.* 帶　　Frisbee〔'frɪzbi〕*n.* 飛盤
play〔ple〕*v.* 玩；播放（音樂）
okay〔'o'ke〕*adv.* 好的（= *OK*）
game〔gem〕*n.* 遊戲　　music〔'mjuzɪk〕*n.* 音樂

27. (**B**)　M：I'd like two tickets, please.

W：For which show, sir?

M：The third one — at 7:30.

W：That will be 400 dollars.

Question：What are the tickets for?

A.　They are 400 dollars.

B.　They are for the 7:30 show.

C.　They are for three people.

* ***would like*** 想要（= *want*）
ticket〔'tɪkɪt〕*n.* 票
which〔hwɪtʃ〕*adj.* 哪一個　　show〔ʃo〕*n.* 表演
for〔fɔr〕*prep.* …用（表用途）
third〔θɝd〕*adj.* 第三的　　dollar〔'dɑlɚ〕*n.* 元

28. (**A**)　M：Do you often take the subway?

　　　　W：Yes.　I take it every day to work.

　　　　M：How long does it take?

　　　　W：Only ten minutes.

　　Question：How often does the woman use the
　　　　　　　subway?

　　A.　At least five days a week.

　　B.　Every ten minutes.

　　C.　As long as it is possible.

* often〔'ɔfən〕*adv.* 經常

　take〔tek〕*v.* 搭乘（交通工具）

　subway〔'sʌbˏwe〕*n.* 地下鐵

　How long ~? ~多久？

　take〔tek〕*v.* 花費（時間）

　only〔'onlɪ〕*adv.* 只有　　minute〔'mɪnɪt〕*n.* 分鐘

　How often ~? ~多久一次？

　use〔juz〕*v.* 使用；利用　　***at least*** 至少

　five days a week 一星期五天

　every ten minutes 每隔十分鐘

　as long as 只要

　possible〔'pɑsəbl̩〕*adj.* 可能的

29. (**C**) M：Do you know how to ride a horse?

W：No. I've never even touched one.

M：They offer horseback riding at the hotel. Why not give it a try?

W：No way! I don't want to fall off and break my neck.

Question：Why won't the woman ride a horse?

A. She does not like to touch animals.

B. She broke her neck.

C. She is afraid that she will get hurt.

* ride〔raɪd〕v. 騎   horse〔hɔrs〕n. 馬
  never〔'nɛvɚ〕adv. 從未
  even〔'ivən〕adv. 甚至
  touch〔tʌtʃ〕v. 觸摸   offer〔'ɔfɚ〕v. 提供
  horseback〔'hɔrs,bæk〕n. 馬背
  horseback riding 騎馬
  hotel〔ho'tɛl〕n. 旅館
  Why not + V. ~? 為何不~？（表提議）
  give it a try 試看看   **No way!** 絕不！
  fall off 跌落   break〔brek〕v. 折斷
  neck〔nɛk〕n. 脖子
  animal〔'ænəml̩〕n. 動物
  afraid〔ə'fred〕adj. 害怕的   **get hurt** 受傷

30. (**B**) M：Do you think I should buy this coat?

W：I thought you wanted a brown one.

M：I do, but this one is on sale.

W：I think you should wait until you find one you really like.

Question：What did the woman advise the man to do?

A. Buy the coat even if he doesn't like it.

B. Buy a brown coat.

C. Buy the cheapest coat.

* think〔θɪŋk〕v. 認為 (三態變化為：think-thought- thought)
  should〔ʃud〕aux. 應該　　buy〔baɪ〕v. 買
  coat〔kot〕n. 外套　　want〔wɑnt〕v. 想要
  brown〔braun〕adj. 棕色的　　*on sale* 特價；拍賣
  wait〔wet〕v. 等待　　until〔ən'tɪl〕prep. 直到
  find〔faɪnd〕v. 找到　　really〔'rɪəlɪ〕adv. 真正地
  like〔laɪk〕v. 喜歡　　advise〔əd'vaɪz〕v. 建議
  even if 即使
  cheapest〔'tʃipɪst〕adj. 最便宜的 (cheap 的最高級)

全民英語能力分級檢定測驗
初級測驗⑫

本測驗分三部份，全為三選一之選擇題，每部份各 10 題，共 30 題，作答時間約 20 分鐘。

第一部份：看圖辨義

本部份共 10 題，試題冊上每題有一個圖片，請聽錄音機播出一個相關的問題，與 A、B、C 三個英語敘述後，選一個與所看到圖片最相符的答案，並在答案紙上相對的圓圈內塗黑作答。每題播出一遍，問題及選項均不印在試題冊上。

例：（看）

（聽）

Look at the picture. How much is the hamburger?

A. It's eighty dollars.
B. It's fifty-five dollars.
C. It's eighteen dollars.

正確答案為 **A**

Questions 1

Question 2

Question 3

Questions 4

Question 5

請 翻 頁 ◀▮▭⟹

Question 6

Question 7

Question 8

Question 9

Question 10

請 翻 頁 ▯▭⟹

第二部份： 問答

　　　　本部份共 10 題，每題錄音機會播出一個問句或直述句，
　　　　每題播出一次，聽後請從試題冊上 A、B、C 三個選項
　　　　中，選出一個最適合的回答或回應，並在答案紙上塗黑
　　　　作答。

　　　　例：

　　　（聽）　Good morning, Kevin. How are you?

　　　（看）　A. I'm fine, thank you.
　　　　　　　B. I'm in the living room.
　　　　　　　C. My name is Kevin.

　　　　　　　正確答案爲 A

11. A. They work very
       hard.
    B. They stopped my
       cough.
    C. They were made in
       a factory.

12. A. It's very cold.
    B. About two meters.
    C. Yes, it's pretty deep.

13. A. I'm a member of the
       art club.
    B. It meets in room 115.
    C. I have to take seven
       classes.

14. A. That's all right.
       Return it tomorrow.
    B. Thanks, I'd love to.
    C. Sorry. I forgot.

15. A. Yes, it was on the
radio.
   B. No, but I saw it on
TV.
   C. No, I wasn't.

16. A. Wait. I'll get a
flashlight.
   B. Don't worry. It
hasn't gone far.
   C. I can't see it.

17. A. Would you like it
toasted?
   B. I'd rather have coffee.
   C. Hot or iced?

18. A. I'm sorry, but I don't
know where we are.
   B. There must have
been an accident
somewhere.
   C. Where do you want
to go?

19. A. It's chocolate.
   B. Yes, it is.
   C. My sister's.

20. A. Yes, to Australia.
   B. Dial zero first.
   C. No, I've never left
the country.

請 翻 頁

第三部份： 簡短對話

　　本部份共 10 題，每題錄音機會播出一段對話及一個相關的問題，每題播出兩次，聽後請從試題冊上 A、B、C 三個選項中，選出一個最適合的回答，並在答案紙上塗黑作答。

例：

（聽）(Woman)　Good afternoon, …Mr. Davis?

　　　(Man)　　Yes.　I have an appointment with Dr. Sanders at two o'clock.　My son Tommy has a fever.

　　　(Woman)　Oh, that's too bad.　Well, please have a seat, Mr. Davis.　Dr. Sanders will be right with you.

　　　Question:　Where did this conversation take place?

（看）A.　In a post office.

　　　B.　In a restaurant.

　　　C.　In a doctor's office.

　　　正確答案為 C

21. A. They will land in
Kaohsiung.

B. They will change their
course.

C. They will change planes.

22. A. They will buy some
flour.

B. They will make a cake
at home.

C. They will buy a cake.

23. A. The movie might be
good.

B. They should not see the
movie.

C. She should not read the
newspaper anymore.

24. A. She had stayed
there for one year.

B. She missed her
home.

C. Her brother told
her to come home.

25. A. She cannot go to
university.

B. She will go to two
universities.

C. She does not know
which university
she will go to.

請 翻 頁 ▯⟹

26. A. She will eat dinner
    soon.
  B. She is trying to lose
    weight.
  C. She does not want
    to eat cookies for
    dinner.

27. A. She thinks the
    newspaper printed
    the wrong price.
  B. She thinks the
    computer may be
    damaged.
  C. She thinks the
    computer is too
    expensive.

28. A. On the fourteenth.
  B. Two days before the
    woman's trip to Hong
    Kong.
  C. On the second day of
    the woman's trip.

29. A. The woman's
    temperature.
  B. The woman's health.
  C. The weather.

30. A. He was not careful.
  B. To let the mosquitoes
    in.
  C. In order to go back
    out.

初級英語聽力檢定⑫詳解

第一部份

Look at the picture for question 1.

1. (**B**) What does the lady have on her arm?
   A. It is an umbrella.　　B. It is a bag.
   C. It is a blouse.

   * lady〔'ledɪ〕*n.* 女士　　arm〔ɑrm〕*n.* 手臂
     umbrella〔ʌm'brɛlə〕*n.* 雨傘　　bag〔bæg〕*n.* 提袋
     blouse〔blauz〕*n.* 女用上衣

Look at the picture for question 2.

2. (**A**) How is the fruit?
   A. It is sour.　　　　B. It is an apple.
   C. She is biting it.

   * fruit〔frut〕*n.* 水果　　sour〔saur〕*adj.* 酸的
     bite〔baɪt〕*v.* 咬 (三態變化為 : bite-bit-bitten)

Look at the picture for question 3.

3. (**B**) Who is in the picture?
   A. A mouth and a hand.
   B. A patient and a dentist.
   C. In the office.

   * picture〔'pɪktʃɚ〕*n.* 圖畫　　mouth〔mauθ〕*n.* 嘴巴
     hand〔hænd〕*n.* 手　　patient〔'peʃənt〕*n.* 病人
     dentist〔'dɛntɪst〕*n.* 牙醫　　office〔'ɔfɪs〕*n.* 辦公室

Look at the picture for question 4.

4. (**C**) What is the man going to do?

    A. Burn a cigarette.

    B. Light the match.

    C. Smoke a pipe.

    * burn〔bɜn〕*v.* 燃燒

        cigarette〔͵sɪgəˊrɛt, ˊsɪgə͵rɛt〕*n.* 香煙

        light〔laɪt〕*v.* 點燃   match〔mætʃ〕*n.* 火柴

        smoke〔smok〕*v.* 抽（煙）   pipe〔paɪp〕*n.* 煙斗

Look at the picture for question 5.

5. (**A**) What is the boy looking for?

    A. The correct answer.

    B. A beautiful girl.

    C. A cheater.

    * *look for* 尋找   correct〔kəˊrɛkt〕*adj.* 正確的

        answer〔ˊænsɚ〕*n.* 答案

        beautiful〔ˊbjutəfəl〕*adj.* 美麗的

        cheater〔ˊtʃitɚ〕*n.* 騙子

Look at the picture for question 6.

6. (**B**) Who is in the shower?

    A. The bathroom.   B. A woman.

    C. It is hot.

    * shower〔ˊʃauɚ〕*n.* 淋浴   *be in the shower* 在淋浴

        bathroom〔ˊbæθ͵rum〕*n.* 浴室   hot〔hɑt〕*adj.* 熱的

Look at the picture for question 7.

7. (**C**) Where did she buy it?

    A. She bought some bread.

    B. He is a baker.

    C. In the bakery.

    * buy〔baɪ〕v. 買（三態變化爲：buy-bought-bought）
       bread〔brɛd〕n. 麵包　　baker〔'bekɚ〕n. 麵包師傅
       bakery〔'bekərɪ〕n. 麵包店

Look at the picture for question 8.

8. (**C**) Why is she resting?

    A. In order to smoke.

    B. It is too hot.

    C. She has a fever.

    * rest〔rɛst〕v. 休息　　***in order to*** ~　爲了要~
       smoke〔smok〕v. 抽煙　　fever〔'fivɚ〕n. 發燒
       have a fever 發燒

Look at the picture for question 9.

9. (**A**) What does the man want?

    A. A new job.

    B. He likes engineers.

    C. He is an engineer.

    * job〔dʒɑb〕n. 工作　　like〔laɪk〕v. 喜歡
       engineer〔͵ɛndʒə'nɪr〕n. 工程師

Look at the picture for question 10.

10. (**B**) What is speeding?
    A. Over 100kph.
    B. An ambulance.
    C. Yes, he is.

    * speed〔spid〕v. 超速行駛
    over〔'ovə〕prep. 超過 (= more than)
    kph 公里／小時；時速⋯公里 (= kilometer per hour)
    ambulance〔'æmbjələns〕n. 救護車

第二部份

11. (**B**) How did those pills work?
    A. They work very hard.
    B. They stopped my cough.
    C. They were made in a factory.

    * pill〔pɪl〕n. 藥丸   work〔wɜk〕v.（藥）有效；工作
    hard〔hɑrd〕adv. 努力地   stop〔stɑp〕v. 止住
    cough〔kɔf〕n. 咳嗽   make〔mek〕v. 製造
    factory〔'fæktrɪ〕n. 工廠

12. (**B**) How deep is the water in the swimming pool?
    A. It's very cold.
    B. About two meters.
    C. Yes, it's pretty deep.

    * deep〔dip〕adj. 深的   *swimming pool* 游泳池
    cold〔kold〕adj. 冷的   meter〔'mitə〕n. 公尺
    pretty〔'prɪtɪ〕adv. 非常

13. (**A**) Do you belong to any clubs at school?

    A. I'm a member of the art club.

    B. It meets in room 115.

    C. I have to take seven classes.

    * ***belong to*** 屬於   club〔klʌb〕*n.* 社團

    member〔'mɛmbɚ〕*n.* 成員   art〔ɑrt〕*adj.* 藝術的

    meet〔mit〕*v.* 集合   take〔tek〕*v.* 修（課）

    class〔klæs〕*n.* 課程

14. (**C**) Did you bring that book you borrowed from me?

    A. That's all right. Return it tomorrow.

    B. Thanks, I'd love to.

    C. Sorry. I forgot.

    * bring〔brɪŋ〕*v.* 帶來   ***borrow from*** ～ 從～借來

    That's all right. 沒關係   return〔rɪ'tɝn〕*v.* 歸還

    would love to V. 想要（= *would like to V.*）

    forget〔fɚ'gɛt〕*v.* 忘記

15. (**B**) Did you read the news about the election?

    A. Yes, it was on the radio.

    B. No, but I saw it on TV.

    C. No, I wasn't.

    * read〔rid〕*v.* 讀   news〔njuz〕*n.* 新聞

    election〔ɪ'lɛkʃən〕*n.* 選舉

    radio〔'redɪ,o〕*n.* 廣播

16. (**A**)　The electricity has gone out again!

    A.　Wait.　I'll get a flashlight.

    B.　Don't worry.　It hasn't gone far.

    C.　I can't see it.

    * electricity〔ɪ,lɛk'trɪsətɪ〕*n.* 電　***go out*** 熄滅；停止運轉
　　　again〔ə'gɛn〕*adv.* 再一次　　wait〔wet〕*v.* 等待
　　　get〔gɛt〕*v.* 去拿　　flashlight〔'flæʃ,laɪt〕*n.* 手電筒
　　　worry〔'wɝɪ〕*v.* 擔心　　far〔fɑr〕*adv.* 遠地

17. (**C**)　Please bring me some tea.

    A.　Would you like it toasted?

    B.　I'd rather have coffee.

    C.　Hot or iced?

    * bring〔brɪŋ〕*v.* 帶（東西）來（給某人）
　　　tea〔ti〕*n.* 茶　　***would like*** 想要（ = *want* ）
　　　toast〔tost〕*v.* 烤　　***would rather V.*** 寧願～
　　　have〔hæv〕*v.* 吃；喝　　coffee〔'kɔfɪ〕*n.* 咖啡
　　　hot〔hɑt〕*adj.* 熱的　　iced〔aɪst〕*adj.* 冰過的

*18. (**B**)　Why is the traffic so bad today?

    A.　I'm sorry, but I don't know where we are.

    B.　There must have been an accident somewhere.

    C.　Where do you want to go?

    * traffic〔'træfɪk〕*n.* 交通　　bad〔bæd〕*adj.* 不好的
　　　must〔mʌst〕*aux.* 一定
　　　accident〔'æksədənt〕*n.* 意外
　　　somewhere〔'sʌm,hwɛr〕*adv.* 在某處

19. (**C**) Whose birthday is it?

    A. It's chocolate.

    B. Yes, it is.

    C. My sister's.

    * whose〔huz〕*pron.* 誰的（當形容詞用）

    birthday〔'bɝθ,de〕*n.* 生日

    chocolate〔'tʃɔkəlɪt〕*n.* 巧克力

20. (**A**) Did you make any international calls?

    A. Yes, to Australia.

    B. Dial zero first.

    C. No, I've never left the country.

    * ***make a call*** 打電話

    international〔,ɪntɚ'næʃənl̩〕*adj.* 國際的

    Australia〔ɔ'streljə〕*n.* 澳洲

    dial〔'daɪəl〕*v.* 撥（電話號碼）   zero〔'zɪro〕*n.* 零

    first〔fɝst〕*adv.* 首先   never〔'nɛvɚ〕*adv.* 從未

    leave〔liv〕*v.* 離開   country〔'kʌntrɪ〕*n.* 國家；國

第三部份

21. (**A**) M：The weather is bad in Taipei, so we cannot land there.

    W：So what will happen?

    M：The pilot has changed course for Kaohsiung.

    Question：What will happen?

A. They will land in Kaohsiung.

B. They will change their course.

C. They will change planes.

* weather〔'wεðə〕*n.* 天氣　　bad〔bæd〕*adj.* 不好的
　Taipei〔'taɪ'pe〕*n.* 台北　　land〔lænd〕*v.* 降落
　happen〔'hæpən〕*v.* 發生　　pilot〔'paɪlət〕*n.* 飛行員
　change〔tʃendʒ〕*v.* 改變　　course〔kors〕*n.* 航線；路線
　Kaohsiung〔'gɑʊ'ʃjʊŋ〕*n.* 高雄　　plane〔plen〕*n.* 飛機

22. (**C**)　M：We need to buy some flour if we want to make a cake.

W：Why don't we just buy one instead?

M：But a homemade cake means more.

W：He is only five years old. It won't matter.

M：You're right. Let's buy one.

Question：What will they do?

A. They will buy some flour.

B. They will make a cake at home.

C. They will buy a cake.

* need〔nid〕*v.* 需要　　flour〔flaʊr〕*n.* 麵粉
　make〔mek〕*v.* 製作　　cake〔kek〕*n.* 蛋糕
　Why don't～? 爲何不～?（表提議）
　just〔dʒʌst〕*adv.* 就…（委婉的祈使語氣）
　instead〔ɪn'stɛd〕*adv.* 作爲代替
　homemade〔'hom'med〕*adj.* 自製的
　mean more 更有意義　　***～years old*** ～歲
　It won't matter. 那沒關係；那不重要。
　matter〔'mætə〕*v.* 事關重大；有問題（用於否定、疑問句）
　right〔raɪt〕*adj.* 對的

23. (**A**) M：Let's go see that new movie.

W：I heard it wasn't very good.

M：Where did you hear that?

W：It was in the newspaper.

M：Well, you can't believe everything you read.

Question：What does the man mean?

A. The movie might be good.

B. They should not see the movie.

C. She should not read the newspaper anymore.

* go to V. 在口語上，有時 to 可以省略，或者用 go and V.。
movie ('muvɪ) n. 電影　　hear (hɪr) v. 聽說
newspaper ('njuz,pepɚ) n. 報紙　　believe (bɪ'liv) v. 相信
everything ('ɛvrɪ,θɪŋ) pron. 一切事物
anymore ('ɛnɪ,mor) adv. 再也 (不) (用於否定句)

24. (**B**) M：I heard Julie just returned from the States.

W：What? She was supposed to stay there for a whole
　　 year.

M：Her brother said she got homesick.

Question：Why did Julie return?

A. She had stayed there for one year.

B. She missed her home.

C. Her brother told her to come home.

* just (dʒʌst) adv. 才；剛剛　　return (rɪ'tɜn) v. 返回
the States 美國　　*be supposed to V.* 應該~
stay (ste) v. 停留　　for (fɔr) prep. 在~期間 (一直)
whole (hol) adj. 整個的　　homesick ('hom,sɪk) adj. 想家的
get homesick 想家　　miss (mɪs) v. 想念

25. (**C**)　M：Have you been accepted by a university yet?

W：Yes.　Two have accepted me.

M：That's great.　Which one will you go to?

W：I can't decide.

Question：What is true about the woman?

　A.　She cannot go to university.

　B.　She will go to two universities.

　C.　She does not know which university she will go to.

* accept〔ək'sɛpt〕v. 接受
　university〔,junə'vɝsətɪ〕n. 大學
　yet〔jɛt〕adv. 已經（用於疑問句）
　That's great. 那眞是太棒了。
　which〔hwɪtʃ〕adj. 哪一個
　decide〔dɪ'saɪd〕v. 決定　　true〔tru〕adj. 正確的

26. (**A**)　M：Please have a cookie.

W：Thank you, but I can't.

M：Don't tell me you're on a diet!

W：No.　But if I eat now, I won't be hungry for dinner.

Question：Why didn't the woman eat a cookie?

　A.　She will eat dinner soon.

　B.　She is trying to lose weight.

　C.　She does not want to eat cookies for dinner.

* have〔hæv〕v. 吃　　cookie〔'kʊkɪ〕n. 餅乾
　on a diet 節食中　　hungry〔'hʌŋgrɪ〕adj. 飢餓的
　dinner〔'dɪnɚ〕n. 晚餐；正餐　　soon〔sun〕adv. 馬上
　try〔traɪ〕v. 試著　　***lose weight*** 減肥

27. (**B**)　M：I saw an advertisement for a used computer.

　　　　W：How much does it cost?

　　　　M：Only 500 dollars!

　　　　W：Be careful.　There might be something wrong
　　　　　　with it.

　　　Question：What does the woman think?

　　　A.　She thinks the newspaper printed the wrong price.

　　　B.　She thinks the computer may be damaged.

　　　C.　She thinks the computer is too expensive.

　　　* see〔si〕*v.* 看見（三態變化爲：see-saw-seen）
　　　　advertisement〔͵ædvɚ'taɪzmənt〕*n.* 廣告
　　　　used〔juzd〕*adj.* 二手的；用過的
　　　　computer〔kəm'pjutɚ〕*n.* 電腦
　　　　cost〔kɔst〕*v.* 值…（錢）　　***Be careful.*** 小心。
　　　　there might be ~ 也許有~
　　　　something wrong with ~ ~有狀況；~有問題
　　　　think〔θɪŋk〕*v.* 認爲　　print〔prɪnt〕*v.* 印刷
　　　　wrong〔rɔŋ〕*adj.* 錯誤的　　price〔praɪs〕*n.* 價錢
　　　　may〔me〕*aux.* 也許；可能　　damage〔'dæmɪdʒ〕*v.* 損害
　　　　expensive〔ɪk'spɛnsɪv〕*adj.* 昂貴的

28. (**B**)　M：When are you leaving for Hong Kong?

　　　　W：On the fourteenth.

　　　　M：That's in two days!　Are you excited?

　　　　W：Sure.

　　　Question：When did this conversation take place?

A. On the fourteenth.

B. Two days before the woman's trip to Hong Kong.

C. On the second day of the woman's trip.

* ***leave for*** 動身前往　　***Hong Kong*** 香港

　fourteenth〔for'tinθ〕*n.* 十四日

　in two days 再過兩天

　excited〔ɪk'saɪtɪd〕*adj.* 興奮的　　sure〔ʃʊr〕*adv.* 當然

　conversation〔͵kɑnvə'seʃən〕*n.* 對話

　take place 發生　　trip〔trɪp〕*n.* 旅行

　second〔'sɛkənd〕*adj.* 第二的

29. (**C**)　M : What is the temperature?

　　　W : It's 28 right now, but it may be as high as 35 this
　　　　　afternoon.

　　　M : Wow!　That's really hot.

　　　W : Yeah.　I think I'll stay inside where it's cool.

　　　Question : What are they talking about?

　　　A. The woman's temperature.

　　　B. The woman's health.

　　　C. The weather.

* temperature〔'tɛmprətʃɚ〕*n.* 溫度；體溫

　right now 現在　　***as…as~*** 和～一樣…

　wow〔waʊ〕*interj.* 哇；噢！（表示驚訝等的叫聲）

　really〔'riəlɪ〕*adv.* 真正地　　hot〔hɑt〕*adj.* 熱的

　yeah〔jæ, jɛ〕*adv.* 是的（= *yes*）　　stay〔ste〕*v.* 停留

　inside〔'ɪn'saɪd〕*adv.* 在室內　　cool〔kul〕*adj.* 涼爽的

　talk about 談論　　health〔hɛlθ〕*n.* 健康

30. (**A**)　M：Hey, there are a lot of mosquitoes in here.

W：Oh, look!　The back door is open.

M：Sorry.　I guess I didn't close it carefully.

Question：Why did the man leave the door open?

A.　He was not careful.

B.　To let the mosquitoes in.

C.　In order to go back out.

* hey〔he〕 *interj.* 嘿（引起注意、表驚訝等的叫聲）

mosquito〔mə'skito〕 *n.* 蚊子

ho〔o〕 *interj.* 噢（表示驚訝等的叫聲）

look〔lʊk〕 *v.* 看；瞧（在此當感歎詞，用以引起注意）

back〔bæk〕 *adj.* 後面的　*adv.* 向後面

open〔'opən〕 *adj.* 開著的

guess〔gɛs〕 *v.* 猜想；想　　close〔kloz〕 *v.* 關上

carefully〔'kɛrfəlɪ〕 *adv.* 小心地

leave〔liv〕 *v.* 使（人、物）處於（某種狀態）

careful〔'kɛrfəl〕 *adj.* 小心的

let〔lɛt〕 *v.* 讓　　 ***in order to*** 為了～

In order to go back out. 為了要再出去。（表從外面回來，

待會還要再出門。）

附錄

全民英語能力分級檢定測驗簡介

　　「全民英語能力分級檢定測驗」（General English Proficiency Test），簡稱「全民英檢」（GEPT），旨在提供我國各階段英語學習者一公平、可靠、具效度之英語能力評量工具，測驗對象包括在校學生及一般社會人士，可做為學習成果檢定、教學改進及公民營機構甄選人才等之參考。

　　本測驗為標準參照測驗（criterion-referenced test），參考當前我國英語教育體制，制定分級標準，整套系統共分五級——初級（Elementary）、中級（Intermediate）、中高級（High-Intermediate）、高級（Advanced）、優級（Superior）。每級訂有明確能力標準（詳見表一綜合能力說明），報考者可依英語能力選擇適當級數報考，每級均包含聽、說、讀、寫四項完整的測驗，通過所報考級數的能力標準即可取得該級的合格證書。各級命題設計均參考目前各階段英語教育之課程大綱及相關教材之內容分析，期能符合國內各階段英語教育的需求、反應本土的生活經驗與特色。

「全民英語能力檢定分級測驗」各級綜合能力說明　　《表一》

級數	綜　合　能　力	備　　　註	
初級	通過初級測驗者具有基礎英語能力，能理解和使用淺易日常用語，英語能力相當於國中畢業者。	建議下列人員宜具有該級英語能力	一般行政助理、維修技術人員、百貨業、餐飲業、旅館業或觀光景點服務人員、計程車駕駛等。
中級	通過中級測驗者具有使用簡單英語進行日常生活溝通的能力，英語能力相當於高中職畢業者。		一般行政、業務、技術、銷售人員、護理人員、旅館、飯店接待人員、總機人員、警政人員、旅遊從業人員等。
中高級	通過中高級測驗者英語能力逐漸成熟，應用的領域擴大，雖有錯誤，但無礙溝通，英語能力相當於大學非英語主修系所畢業者。		商務、企劃人員、祕書、工程師、研究助理、空服人員、航空機師、航管人員、海關人員、導遊、外事警政人員、新聞從業人員、資訊管理人員等。

級數	綜　合　能　力		備　　　　註	
高級	通過高級測驗者英語流利順暢，僅有少許錯誤，應用能力擴及學術或專業領域，英語能力相當於國內大學英語主修系所或曾赴英語系國家大學或研究所進修並取得學位者。	建議下列人員宜具有該級英語能力	高級商務人員、協商談判人員、英語教學人員、研究人員、翻譯人員、外交人員、國際新聞從業人員等。	
優級	通過優級測驗者的英語能力接近受過高等教育之母語人士，各種場合均能使用適當策略作最有效的溝通。		專業翻譯人員、國際新聞特派人員、外交官員、協商談判主談人員等。	

初級英語能力測驗簡介

I. 通過初級檢定者的英語能力

聽	説	讀	寫
能聽懂簡易的英語句子、對話及故事。	能簡單地自我介紹並以簡易英語對答；能朗讀簡易文章。	能瞭解簡易英語對話、短文、故事及書信的內容；能看懂常用的標示。	能寫簡單的英語句子及段落。

II. 測 驗 內 容

測驗項目	初 試			複 試
	聽力測驗	閱讀能力測驗	寫作能力測驗	口說能力測驗
總題數	30	35	16	18
作答時間 / 分鐘	約 20	35	40	約 10
測驗內容	看圖辨義 問答 簡短對話	詞彙和結構 段落填空 閱讀理解	單句寫作 段落寫作	複誦 朗讀句子與短文 回答問題

　　聽力及閱讀能力測驗成績採標準計分方式，60分為平均數，滿分120分。寫作及口說能力測驗成績採整體式評分，使用級分制，分為0～5級分，再轉換成百分制。各項成績通過標準如下：

III. 成績計算及通過標準

初　　試	通過標準 / 滿分	複　　試	通過標準 / 滿分
聽力測驗	80 / 120 分		
閱讀能力測驗	80 / 120 分	口說能力測驗	80 / 100 分
寫作能力測驗	70 / 100 分		

IV. 寫作能力測驗級分說明

第一部份：單句寫作級分說明

級　分	説　　　　明
2	正確無誤。
1	有誤，但重點結構正確。
0	錯誤過多、未答、等同未答。

第二部份：段落寫作級分說明

級　分	説　　　　明
5	正確表達題目之要求；文法、用字等幾乎無誤。
4	大致正確表達題目之要求；文法、用字等有誤，但不影響讀者之理解。
3	大致回答題目之要求，但未能完全達意；文法、用字等有誤，稍影響讀者之理解。
2	部份回答題目之要求，表達上有令人不解/誤解之處；文法、用字等皆有誤，讀者須耐心解讀。
1	僅回答1個問題或重點；文法、用字等錯誤過多，嚴重影響讀者之理解。
0	未答、等同未答。

各部份題型之題數、級分及總分計算公式：

分項測驗	測驗題型	各部份題數	每題級分	佔總分比重
第一部份：單句寫作	A. 句子改寫	5題	2分	50％
	B. 句子合併	5題	2分	
	C. 重組	5題	2分	
第二部份：段落寫作	看圖表寫作	1篇	5分	50％
總分計算公式	公式：{(第一部份得分/30)＋(第二部份得分/5)}×50 例：第一部份各項得分　A－8分 　　　　　　　　　　　　B－10分 　　　　　　　　　　　　C－8分 8+10+8=26 三項加總第一部份得分 － 26分 第二部份得分 － 4分 依公式計算如下： {(26/30)＋(4/5)}×50=83　該考生得分83分			

　　凡應考且合乎規定者一律發給成績單。初試及複試各項測驗成績通過者，發給合格證書，本測驗成績紀錄保存兩年。

　　初試通過者，可於一年內單獨報考複試，得重複報考。惟複試一旦通過，即不得再報考。

　　已通過本英檢測驗初級，一年內不得再報考同級數之測驗。違反本規定報考者，其應試資格將被取消，且不退費。

（以上資料取自「全民英檢學習網站」http://www.gept.org.tw）

劉毅英文初級英檢模考班

I. **上課時間：** 每週日下午 2：00～5：00

II. **上課方式：** 完全比照財團法人語言訓練中心所做「初級英語檢定測驗」初試標準。分為聽力測驗、閱讀能力測驗、及寫作能力測驗三部分。每次上課舉行 70 分鐘的模擬考，包含 30 題聽力測驗，35 題詞彙結構、段落填空、閱讀理解、及 16 題單句寫作、及一篇段落寫作。考完試後立即講解，馬上釐清所有問題。

III. **收費標準：** （含代辦初級檢定考試報名及簡章費用）

期　數	3個月	6個月	1年保證班
週　數	12週	24週	48週
費　用	5800元	9800元	14800元

※ 1. 劉毅英文同學優待 *1000* 元。

　 2. 保證班若無通過，免費贈送一年課程。

IV. **報名贈書：** 初級英檢全套書籍

報名立刻開始背誦「初級英檢公佈字彙①－⑩」

劉毅英文・毅志文理補習班（兒美、國中、高中、成人班、全民英檢代辦報名）

班址：台北市許昌街 17 號 6 F（火車站前・壽德大樓）　☎ (02) 2389-5212

本書製作過程

　　本書是由美籍老師 Laura E. Stewart 負責編寫所有內容，蔡惠婷小姐負責整理資料，並加上註釋。特別感謝謝靜芳老師再三仔細校訂，白雪嬌小姐負責封面設計，黃淑貞小姐負責版面設計及編排。

||||||||||||||●學習出版公司門市部●||||||||||||||||

台北地區： 台北市許昌街 10 號 2 樓　TEL：(02)2331-4060・2331-9209
台中地區： 台中市綠川東街 32 號 8 樓 23 室
　　　　　 TEL：(04)2223-2838

||||||||||||||||||||||||||||||||||||||||||||||||

初級英語聽力檢定⑤

主　　　編 / 劉　毅
發　行　所 / 學習出版有限公司　　　　　☎ (02) 2704-5525
郵 撥 帳 號 / 0512727-2 學習出版社帳戶
登　記　證 / 局版台業 2179 號
印　刷　所 / 裕強彩色印刷有限公司
台 北 門 市 / 台北市許昌街 10 號 2 F　　　☎ (02) 2331-4060・2331-9209
台 中 門 市 / 台中市綠川東街 32 號 8 F 23 室　☎ (04) 2223-2838
台灣總經銷 / 紅螞蟻圖書有限公司　　　　☎ (02) 2795-3656
美國總經銷 / Evergreen Book Store　　　☎ (818) 2813622
本公司網址　www.learnbook.com.tw
電 子 郵 件　learnbook@learnbook.com.tw

售價：新台幣一百八十元正
2005 年 11 月 1 日一版二刷

ISBN 957-519-831-X